D1176109

AN ARMFUL
OF
WARM GIRL

AN ARMFUL
OF
WARM GIRL

by W. M. Spackman

ALFRED A. KNOPF

NEW YORK

1978

THIS IS A BORZOI BOOK

PUBLISHED BY ALFRED A. KNOPF, INC.

An Armful of Warm Girl was originally published in *Canto Review of the Arts,* Summer 1977.

Library of Congress Cataloging in Publication Data

Spackman, William Mode [date]
An armful of warm girl.

"Originally published in Canto review of the arts, summer 1977."
I.   Title.
PZ4.S732Arm   1978   [PS3569.P3]   813'.5'4
77-21170   ISBN 0-394-50000-8

Manufactured in the United States of America

First Edition

DIS MÂNIBVS
ALFREDI YOUNG FISHER
COMMILITONIS

AN ARMFUL
OF
WARM GIRL

He was born pretty damn' irked, with a Caldwell's spoon in his mouth, to a family of short-tempered Philadelphia-Quaker private bankers, on a stifling country-summer morning in 1909. Or a Bailey Banks & Biddle spoon, what difference does it make, father could've bought and sold 'em both twice over. Weighed twelve pounds; they all did then; grew up big too. And in due course graduated from Princeton in the Class of 1931, though who didn't.

Though as it happens only just graduated, having got himself under sentence of rustication, spring of his junior year, for half breaking a classmate's back after a lush June wedding at Trinity. In a stripped and bare-handed midnight duel, of all fool things!—dim starlight down by the Lake, grass skiddy with blood and dew, some pre-med classmate standing by and a couple of Virginia classmates for seconds, this fellow-usher having had the incredible damn' taste to describe the bride, mind you the guy's own roommate's girl! as "built like a brick Gertrude Stein." But the common bastard turned out not to be paralyzed, so they dropped the rustication.

Additionally, come to think of it, got his nose broken in the Place du Théâtre in Dijon during his formal grand tour in the summer of '31. Served him right: made some mannerless generalization ("Faut-il quand même qu'on y foute du lait maternel?") on the indiscriminate riches of Burgundian cookery.

Otherwise a life like anybody's—married a delicious Main Line deb; usual children usual love-affairs; succeeded as chairman, at their Bank, his bellowing father. But who wants to bother with this background claptrap? or for that matter like Homer invoke a Muse on the subject-matter of mere size and bad temper, when the point about a protagonist is that here he is here-and-now, this big-boned striding irascible man with his blood-shot and arrogant blue eyes—what's *he* care for his boyhood and the rest of it? Let Freud fuss with all that. Or for variety Aristarchus.

So then this is 1959, and down to business.

On *this* country-summer morning, then (here and now), a summer morning already hot and still, every drowsing green ride of landscape toppling with light, this Nicholas Romney, a Philadelphia private banker aged fifty years or as good as, a Chester County squire now stiff-faced with rage and deep affront, left his inherited groves, his woodland chases, his messuage and out-farms, and in particular his wife, and banged off in his ancient Bentley down his great-grandfather's furlong of carriage-drive toward the outrage of exile in New York.

Having no more than reached a time of life when all he or any man in his senses wanted was to settle down with some agreeable woman or other, at the very least a wife he was used to and fond of—"and the irresponsible bitch *leaves* me!!" he yelled.

So away, alone.

In his meadows, in the flash and dazzle of the morning, his fat black cattle grazed through the jingleweed, his white guineas ran huddling. In his parks of oak and hickory the woods' high crowns discharged their splintered emeralds of light, the dogwoods shook out in flower, pink or cream, their weightless sprays. In his grove his great-grandfather's beeches, nave on nave, shone in their argent elegance, his glossy peacocks straggled, his grandfather's marble folly reared its Palladian ruins, studded with busts of ottocento celebrities, now seriously begrimed. In his box maze glittered the fantailed Cytherean tumbling of his doves.

And all this, by one pretty woman's perversity, now done with, unreal; as lost to him as if by disseizin; plundered; *gone*!

For not twelve hours ago she'd stood cool and tall before him and said in her stylish drawl he didn't expect her to account to him did he? not any longer now surely; or for that matter explain; or in any case expect her to mock ordinary good manners by asking him would he mind? when why pretend he'd in the least mind "beyond the temporary vexation to yourself, Nicholas"—this, if you'll credit such a thing, from a woman he'd thought he'd known every sweet inch of, and for years!

Many years; many happy years, to reckon the plain fact! A whole warm and smiling chronicle, a sentient lifetime. And now here what was she but become this stranger.

Thus then he'd packed and gone.

What with her preposterous "not another day"—fancy making use of such an expression! had she no more sense of prose style than that after a quarter-century of his company?

So like any man in his right mind he ground out between his teeth a discountenanced "Wife wants to go let her by heaven *go,* up to *her* infatuated levity not mine!"

Adding, stunned, "Tired of *me,* can you imagine!" though the emerging fact was, now he'd got around to noticing it—and here was the final disobliging and unnatural affront—as to this requested divorce she never in so many words had told him why!

So this baffled man drove through West Chester and on toward Chester and the ferry dispirited and glaring dismally, his mind as good as vacant apart from the customary interior rodomontade.

For what had he done to be deserted like this, loved her hadn't he? And if not exclusively, still by heaven these many many years! And as much as he or any man had it in him to, hadn't he, all things considered? Well, then!

Or if he'd bored her why not say so!

Though what real likelihood, she hadn't bored *him* had she? Or not much. Or not more than was normal and understood. Or anyhow not bored often, and damned if he'd had the bad breeding to show it in any case. In any case he hadn't held it against her had he? And so at last, muttering complaints by this time at her irresponsible damn' technique of merely handling a husband, this endless confronting him instead of manoeuvring round him nuzzling and femalizing at him like a European woman ("like a *woman* dammit!") he drove onto the ferry.

Where, as it happened, in the car next his there was a delicious-looking girl to stare at.

Who finally smiled at him; so presently drove into New York, where he'd not passed a night in many years, feeling rather less embittered than had promised. And at Veale's Hotel, though now changed from the Thirties almost past his disconcerted recognition, he had a very decent squab, à la Marigny or some such, with a bottle of Hermitage, and half a dozen pretty women in good view—two of whom, a normal enough percentage, ogled him charmingly through drooping lashes.

In fact he felt much better.

So after a nap, fourish or so, he rang up his New York daughter.

"Melissa?"

"Hello?"

"Mélisse how *are* you my sweet baby, regret I've got to inform you at once an infuriating thing's occurred. Matter of fact an outrage, I've been badly ups— "

"I'm terribly sorry but who is this?" she said in her fashionable young voice. "I can hardly—"

"How's that? This is your fathcr!"

"Hello? Hello?"

He blared into the phone, "Now see here Melissa dammit I'm resigned to a few symbolic communication-difficulties of a routine order but by heaven—"

"Why *daddy!*" her pleased voice cried, "why how perfectly, why darling where are you then!"

"What?"

"I mean how blissful hearing you out of the seamless blue like this, where are you phoning *from*?"

"What? I'm at Veale's. Naturally. Where else?"

"Could you speak just a little louder d'you think?"

He shouted *"Can you hear this?"* at her.

"Yes *much* better, where are you?"

"An old-fashioned private hotel called—"

"You're in New York, why daddy what's this!"

"Look, my precious child, if you'll just—"

"Mummy too?"

"No!"

"Oh mummy *not* with you, where's she?"

"How do I know dammit!"

"What, darling?"

He violently announced, "Your unhinged mother's taken it into her head to divorce me, is what!"

"Oh daddy not so loud, I can't hear anything but a sort of bellow."

So he translated down, and into a tone nearer the Horatian irony called for, "Your mother has I regret to say taken it into her pretty head to propose that she divorce me."

"...............*divorce!!*" cried their daughter in accents of shock and universal scandal.

"Yes by god!"

"Oh daddy, oh poor loves!"

"A sheer outrage!" he told her in a despondent roar.

"Yes but daddy but *mummy*!"

"Deliberate affront of a pretty damn' unrefined—"

"But *who* on earth?"

"What?"

"Yes; who in love with; oh hideous!"

"Now what in God's name has love got to do with it!"

"Oh darling don't yell so, getting her divorce *for* I mean. I mean to marry him or whoever."

He snarled, "Your mother has not it appears seen fit to provide me with the customary rival, if you want to know. No doubt flattered herself I'd fling the swine in the pond."

"Pond, daddy?"

"Well, the tenants' pond, what difference does it— Now look here Melissa the point doesn't arise. I've just said. Your mother's not in love with somebody else. Or with anybody, merely doesn't appear to want to live any longer with *me.*"

"There couldn't be some, well, *terribly* stealthy—"

"Now listen to me Melissa—"

"Only pet but nobody *at all*?" wailed the former Miss Romney dismayed.

"The structures of female romanticism aside," her father pronounced testily, "why should there be somebody? Or is the question one one's daughters reply to?"

"What, daddy?"

"What d'ye mean 'what' dammit, anyhow the point's perfectly clear and undebatable: wretched woman doesn't want any longer to be married to anybody. Or so in the absence of any responsible explanation from her I'm forced to conclude. Doesn't anyhow want to live with *me*—can you conceive of such behavior?"

"Now *pet* she must have said!"

"What?"

"Darling *said.*"

"Said what? Said you two girls were both married now (she 'supposed' happily), both married and your brothers at least *in* college, as if that had anything to do with it! When how's anyone know? herself included, for all I— Do you realize that now for weeks on end I'll have to commute down to that root-canal man in West Philadelphia?''

"But darling couldn't you persuade her that a—''

" 'Persuade her'! You out of your pretty senses? If she was done she was done, *I* wasn't going to beseech her to change her mind. Out of *her* senses! As I told her!''

"Oh daddy you yelled at her?''

"Naturally I yelled at her!''

"Oh blessing,'' she mourned, "oh what a thing, oh poor loves; oh just when we *all*.''

"Isn't it though? Isn't it?''

"And all your darling little marottes.''

"My what?''

"Like the peacocks. And great-grandfather's stone poets you were going to have scoured, ah how sad.''

"*Well,*'' he agreed, in unhappy tones.

"Will mummy see to them?''

He cried, "How do I know!''

"And when it's all yours!''

"Now see here my lovely baby, I couldn't in reason throw your da— your poor mother out! Of hearth and home? Limits, I have to assume, even to *my* late-Edwardian attitudes.''

"But I mean it was grandfather's, dearest, *your* father's not mummy's. And great-grandfather's and so forth; why, back and back forever, you're always telling.''

"Now imagine your being concerned!''

"Well but daddy *yes*!''

"Well it is a lovely old place in practice by god isn't it.''

"Why, it's my whole lost sweet growing-up girlhood,'' she laughed, lightly delivering this line at him, as from footlights.

"The groves, the high woods, the light,'' he lamented tenderly, "the eighteenth-century solitudes, why Melissa I was a boy, a tiny child, there.''

"Such dreaming summers; ah, what sweets.''

"Not that you're ever even near the place now particularly,'' he said with sudden deep gloom.

"What? why I *am*!''

"Or really stay.''

"When I was there only this Easter?"

"In what seems long long years."

She was wildly astonished.

He concluded loudly, "*Miss* you in fact, darling child!"

"Well *dearest* then!"

So he mumbled something.

"I mean but *darling* daddy!" she cried. "Why, of *all* the!"

"See something more of you now anyhow, huh. Going to open the little Barrow Street house, all things considered: it's been—"

"But then you can't mean you're settling here then, I mean daddy the 'dower house' and all?"

"Well, for the next few months I—"

"But what can your plans be? why sweetie all your friends are around I thought Philadelphia."

"Now Mélisse," he said, amused, "no more friends than that, good god?"

"But New York! when you haven't *been* in twenty years."

"Seventeen."

"Well, seventeen."

"Must know dozens of people here still. All my old New York girls, for a start."

"Oh daddy seventeen *years*, and married to other people now anyhow, aren't they."

"Married to other people *then*," he snickered.

"Daddy!"

"Ah, well, though," he resumed, in tones of threnody, "You do of course have a point. Seventeen years," he pronounced heavily. "Not even I suppose excluded that some of them may be even dead, poor sweet creatures. Happened to a classmate of mine only day before yesterday."

"What, daddy?"

"Being buried today. Be there for the service too, you know, except for your confounded mother."

"Oh darling someone you knew?"

"Well, no, actually; or anyhow hardly; just another damn' Philadelphia banker. But a member of the Class!" he cried in acute self-pity.

She crooned, "Ah, dearest," rather moved.

"Saw him not forty-eight hours before he died, too, poor guy. Pink and vigorous; absolutely glowing with health."

"Ah daddy."

"Poor guy. Must have had his plans too. Like all of us. Then next day, or the next, quite simply we miss him from the accustomed hill. Ah well. Such a shame, somehow, Melissa."

"Ah but old *sweet*," she grieved.

"Though as it happens," her father said in a different tone altogether, "A complete stuffed shirt actually, if you want the fact of it, bored the blessings out of anybody but his fellow Republicans. Class is full of these well-behaved people, what's Princeton do to 'em? Frightful thing: no real standards, just *behave* well, poor decent amiable dying muggs. Where's the short-tempered Achilles that we knew? Well though here dammit, mustn't keep you with this dismal sort of stuff, when can I see you? By the way how's your husband?" he demanded suddenly. "Marrying these wretched Yale success-boys," he tailed off grumbling.

"Now daddy sssshh, he's lovely."

"Well when can *I* see you!" he cried.

"Why, any time! why *sweetie*!"

"Lunch tomorrow then? Or's dinner better?"

"Well I'm afraid *tomorrow*—"

"Day after, then, huh."

"When if I'd only known you were coming!"

"Weekend then? or that impossible too!"

"Oh daddy I *am* so sorry but the thing is we've got this endlessly long-standing weekend up in Connecticut with—"

"Well then *Monday*!"

"Only don't you see the frightful fact *is* we hadn't actually meant to get back till very possibly— Now look *darling* could you ring up then? when I mean we can keep it open? and find out what you intend *doing*, I mean *here* and so forth! because then we can have you all properly up in full fig and all!"

So he said rather testily he'd give her a ring then, why certainly, be delighted to; and hung up.

Presently he rang first one Princeton son, then the other. Neither of these miserable boys was in, and not one of their clods of roommates either; and his other daughter being that fortnight with her proconsular young husband in Istanbul of all places, he had nothing to do but shave and shower.

Under the razor his face had never glowed with a pinker health. "......poor guy," he muttered elegiacally, slupping the lather around his firm jaw; after a while adding, "Heu, modo tantus, ubi es?" thanks to a decent Classical education.

◆❧◆

So evening came on; and after seventeen years (or even conceding in this case it was twenty) in agreeable expectation he rang up Angelina Hume.

Having first debated aloud with himself, in the clouting torrents of the shower, what pictures of her his memory's eye was actually on, what pageants glimpsed down what flowery perspectives; since otherwise he might just be remembering What's-his-name's gainsboroughization of her in the National Gallery instead. So now in a knotted towel, combed and cologned, he rang her up, in his hand a frayed rectangle of paper he'd kept all these years happily ever after, which once upon a time the two of them had passed back and forth and back and forth, at whatever stuffed bankers' banquet it had been twenty years ago, with her damn' husband (her first one) at the speakers' table and she and Nicholas feeding side by side below the salt an urbane eight inches apart, while scribbling on *this very paper,* here now in his eager hand, their antiphonal enchantment:

— 8 inches much too *far* [his pen had written]

— *Yes!* [had answered her scrawling backhand]

— Don't be monosyllabic, think of synonyms

— *All right—I'll think and what I think is you're adorable—3 syllables—Want more?*

— I want any and *all*

— *I'd like to go make love—All monosyllables—and you* dont *like them?*

— [a crease, his reply illegible; paper rubbed and worn]

— *Come on that wasn't an answer—Write something like I write— Such as you have sweet curls on your head*

('Curls'?) But now anyhow in her 73rd Street palazzo her phone rang and was answered, and he said with smiling anticipation, "Like to speak to Mrs. Hume please; Mr. Romney, tell her."

".....

"Well, be in shortly I presume? ask her if she'll—"

".....

"What? why g— Why that's *extremely disappointing* dammit, where can I reach her then?"

".....

"Can't 'give out' her out-of-town address, what d'ye mean 'out,' dammy I've known your mistress twenty years!"

".....

"Now see here then, where *is* Mrs. Hume?"

".....

" '*In Europe*'!" he exploded.

Wildly staring.

And dressed stunned and speechless.

"Yes *speechless*!" he trumpeted, thrashing his way into a shirt. "Is every unaccountable damn' woman I want to see up to something else by god? A display of insensibility that I—of inconsider— Have they *no* responsi— And where in the name of God are my black socks!" he snarled, flinging the trunk-till onto the bed.

And rooted in vain: wife gone, heartless daughter off weeks on end in some Connecticut commuters' slum with her huge child of a husband, and now for a third, and past any system of probabilities known to man, his own Angelina not even in the same hemisphere! and in a word, "*Deserted* by god!" he shouted at his image in the glass, flailing a fistful of sober ties.

Pulled on his socks muttering, "Been too kind to the finicky bitches, is what," pretty dismally.

For spend your whole self-sacrificing lifetime on 'em, in single-minded devotion mind you! and now here for reward where was he but some hog's-own hotel changed out of all semblance of memory!

The bed not merely too soft but too short!

Yes! and with the plumbing roaring and racketing day and everlasting night!

Yes! and no sooner settle down for a night's decent rest in due course than in all likelihood from some nextdoor room there'd come a rushing and trampling, a delighted nubile screeching, and the hoarse male grunts of Edwardian desire ...

So by *god* he stomped out of his room and down into the bar pretty damn' near speechless again.

And waiting for the first glass of his evening champagne he sat in a corner glaring: one cloyed flitting self-indulgent unreachable female after another, the whole performance beyond belief; and if now like a reasonable man he rang up his angel Victoria Barclay next, what unforeseeable dither of universal disorder mightn't he find there too!

And to cap everything he had to call the gerent over, or whatever the man was, to complain glowering about this champagne, was it ullaged or what? and as the fellow scuttled off for a fresh bottle, snapped after him "Not even your bar's the same!"—this once familiar room changed now as those redecorated hearts; all he'd known vanishing; so that what was there that once had been and still was.

The second glass was better. So he stomped over to the bar glass in hand and lectured the bartender on négociants, vignobles, and the like, with testy brevity.

Or at first brevity; for soon, while having his third glass to exemplify, in warmer detail.

Till ultimately, from the vapors of the fourth or fifth along the now crowded and affronting bar, he strolled forth from their damned din and took the air in an archaizing trance—forth alone, into the murmuring early-summer evening, to pace uptown for a block or two through the tender diamonds of Park Avenue twilight; eye bright enough though the fact was without anybody much now to ogle; and so, rather soon, ah well, back toward Veale's again, under his breath humming Passacaglia With Floy-Floy in amiablest nostalgia; and so to dinner, alone.

Eating which, he recalled other tunes now foundered in time. For example what was that great flabby gullah's name in the Thirties that sang at supper in the Iridium Room? woman had practically no teeth, sang with her great lavender gums somehow, anyway he finished his fruits de mer (they appeared to be done with burnt pernod) humming her famous

> Settin' around in mah underclo'es
> Gettin' a piece o' yo' mind.

Probably extremely talented singer actually technically, wherever now lost or gone.

And over his tournedos recalled a nachtmusik that once upon a time had been composed explicitly for *him*, had it somewhere or other still, must have, mind's eye saw the score with absolute clarity: this hand-inked score. For that sweet creature temporarily his, what had she done but set some verses she found pleased him, as a pavan, some seventeenth-century-sounding thing, Stay Lovely Peasant What Wild Flights Are These—only then the mad angel had inscribed his copy "To Nicholas from his un-fled non-peasant" (a fine piece of embroilment for a wife to find, God help everybody involved!), and what if afterward she had had a final fiery tantrum at him and raged off never to return, had that love been any the less delicious an échange de deux fantaisies?

So he went on, next, to remember (it having come next)—remembered sighing one brief and tender affair with ah, how different an ending, and her last letter he still knew every sad syllable of by heart: *Darling—One of the conditions of maturity is that no one is free to perform heroic rescues. Adieu.*

Thus by dessert why not concede the well-fed melancholy Renaissance point then? *They flee from me that sometyme did me seke* and what man of sense (and with other resources anyhow) would call it unforeseen no matter what the lovely skittish things did or didn't adopt as behavior? including past all reason an adieu.

"When who knows what they may fancy they've set their heat-simple little pink hearts on next goddammit," he complained in mellow affection; and having sent the man for a marc concluded, "Whereas when have *I* by heaven *not* been in love with some agreeable creature or other?" and so, finally, began to laugh.

He'd ring Victoria. First thing in the morning.

And swayed off with dignity to bed.

Next forenoon at a reasonable hour, then, having done the chores (bought black socks in the Grand Central area and then, being thereabouts, dropped in on a banker classmate at the Guaranty and increased his account there substantially, refusing a not only extremely civil but even warmly pressing invitation to lunch while arranging to be put up for a couple of clubs they agreed were suitable, and then dropped in on another classmate at Chase to discuss his Bank's account there and having to plead and smilingly defend a previous lunch engagement in the face of all kinds of friendly importunity, only to find himself proposed for a third club before he got away, and in short was decently treated everywhere and why not), on his way back to Veale's through the sun-flooded haze of late morning stepped into a florist's and had Melissa sent a great swaying tangled armful of city-spring flowers; and so at last, heart brimming with vernal nostalgia, even with libertine hope, rang up Mrs. Barclay after these seventeen years.

"Victoria?"

"Yes?"

"Victoria!"

"Yes who is this please?"

"This is Nicholas; Nicholas Romney."

A charming little diamond of a cry: "Oh Nicholas not you *re*ally not actually oh *no*!"

At that happy voice, that cascade of light and jewelled syllables, like no other woman's ever, what could the man's remembering tongue do? but utter once again, after seventeen years, as of its own seraphic volition, the opening phrases of that incantation known to the two of them alone, exordium once (ah me) to how many an undiscovered dialogue; so he breathed, "Mi vuoi sempre bene?"

And sure enough, heard the sweet antiphonal reproach (as how often, ahimè how long ago), "Nicola, Nicola ... "

Had any man in history ever heard a lovelier voice? He stammered, shaken with delight, "Well then *say*, dammit: mi vuoi bene?"

"Ma se te ne vogl—   Oh no but really Nicholas *fancy* hearing you even over a phone again, how unimaginable! I mean how unimaginably *pleasant*!'' she finished rapidly, in châtelaine tones.

"Se sapessi quanto io—''

"Now Nicholas. After all *this* time after all! We should say 'lei' anyhow, we—''

"It's timeless!''

"—shouldn't even be talking Italian, now you must tell me where you merely *are*,'' she ordered brightly, "why where can you be staying then, oh really what a thing!''

"You pretend you don't even remember how it goes on from there?'' he accused her.

"What, Nicholas? From where? How *what* goes?''

"Angel Victoria, our 'dialogue.' ''

"Oh, that. Oh.''

"What comes after 'ma se te ne voglio.' ''

"Nicholas, I—''

"After you've said 'se te ne voglio!' with that lovely, love-stricken music of reproach in it, remember? What I used to say next?''

"*Really Nicholas!*''

"So you do remember!'' he exulted, with delighted laughter.

"Nicholas I will simply hang up!''

"You do remember, by heaven how could either of us forget!''

"Very easily indeed!'' she said in a tremulous voice, "when after all one hasn't thought of any of it, even, practically, for years.''

"Haven't you?''

"Now Nicholas why on earth should I!''

"But haven't you anyhow?''

"Certainly not!''

"You're a sweet married liar,'' he said amiably. "*I* have.''

"Now Nicholas.''

"By god I have!''

"Yes but never quite enough to make you ever come to see me even, *did* you Nicholas dear!''

He shouted into the phone, "Good god Victoria do you seriously pretend to think with one lovely melting melted atom of you that a single atom of me will ever forget anything about you till the day the last breath sighs out of my body?''

She said, in moved tones, "Such a rhetorical liar, oh Nicholas."

"Calling me 'lei'! As if every nerve in my—"

"Ah Nicholas."

"You even planning to pretend you've forgotten Alassio?"

" ... Ah Nicholas."

"And that hotel in Pisa?"

"Were we ever so frozen anywhere, oh *darling* how cold!"

"Then your damn' husband wired!" he denounced her.

" ... I know."

"Meet him in Geneva or some such place; perfect outrage; you came running up to me across the Piazza dei Cavalieri waving the blackguard's wire—"

She murmured, stricken, "You even remember the piazza's name."

"Didn't you?"

"Oh Nicholas *yes*! But I never thought you would."

"What? Infallible geographic memory, drive you round Rome blindfold, even now."

"Like a homing pigeon, cocchiere mio," she fondly sighed, "only who was it drove us out to lunch at Frascati the noon we ended *up* at Castel Gondolfo?"

"Everything, you remember everything!" he cried out in jubilation.

"Oh Nicholas isn't it suddenly frightening, *I do*!"

So they pronounced each other's names three or four times over in accents of happy lamentation. He then groaned, "When *can* I see you my utter angel?"

"Oh *yes*!"

"No, I said 'when.' "

"What, darling?" she breathed, lost in dream.

"I said, 'I said "wh— " ' *god* Victoria when this absolute minute—"

"Ah I know!"

"Where will you meet me then my angel!"

"So sweet."

"I mean for lunch; today; now."

" ... '*Now*'!" she cried out, as abruptly awoken.

"Dinner tonight then if I have to wait till then!"

At this she uttered a little musical scream of sheer common sense. "Now you can't inform me you're tied up!"

"Oh Nicholas *of course* we're tied up, we're having a—"

"Well then tomorrow!"

"Oh when I so long to see you it's *dementing*, why I've been tied up tomorrow for utter months!" she wailed in star-crossed despair.

"But I—"

"Why, this whole coming weekend for months!"

"Now Victoria how can you!" he expostulated in tones of the most picturesque unhappiness.

"But we're due in Concord then! You don't even know that I have a huge great fifth-former son?"

"Your *son*!" he shouted in affront.

On which she demanded with spirit whether in sixteen years, or in point of fact longer than sixteen years, a heartless expanse of time and she forbore to reckon it, he had even bothered his faithless head to enquire!

So they wrangled gently.

For she told him now she was looking in her book he could see for himself she hadn't two free minutes end to end this whole frenetic coming *week* because of his treatment of her! when what could he merely have expected? when self-evidently she was helpless if he dropped out of any casual cloud! by which time he'd just be back in that dismal Philadelphia long ago again anyhow wouldn't he?

He had therefore to explain to her in outline this vagary of his irresponsible wife's, this divorce, Mrs. Barclay uttering little arpeggios of innocence and concern in comment.

So by god she could see he had no intention whatever of returning to Philadelphia *or* his West Chester place until their lawyers had got every last parochial inequivocation signed and sealed with their interminable crimson wax. Take months. Take a year; so he had to see her at once, surely she saw?

Hadn't he even listened? she'd been telling him till she was hoarse (she cried in a voice of music) that every exhausting minute of her time was already pledged twice over for ten absolute days, when he hadn't even told her where he was putting up, where she could reach him if, because where *was* he? when she was just enmeshed!

He said at Veale's, natur—

His *impossible* self-centered unpractical demands, 'dinner tomorrow' indeed!

He instantly said tea-time.

Was she to fling to the winds her every appointment? every ordered plan she'd made in her book, was he some mere savage?

Absolute Boeotian, he conceded in an ingratiating whine.

Utterly putting out everyone else for a wretched twenty minutes her soft misguided heart might just conceivably—

He gave an enraptured pealing cry.

Well she was *concerned* about him then! she cried out at him, when here he was sounding upset and lonely and she was *fond* of him, did he expect her to deny that? for *old times'* sake she was fond, also his immediately ringing her up about this mad decision of his wife's, well, she was touched, well who wouldn't be touched then! and she felt *sorry* for him so there! she more or less snapped at him in conclusion.

He said she was the uttermost of archangels.

Unless by some chance (she said in a different tone altogether) *he* were the one getting this divorce. He rather than his wife. Something she of course couldn't say, not knowing.

He said certainly not, it—

Or however it was in fact occurring, whatever had taken place, she meant; or possibly was still taking place; he not having yet given her a specific account; or details.

He said what? occur? what'd she mean?

Yes, she meant what had. The particulars.

He said but what was there to 'occur'? woman'd simply walked out on him, not literally of course because she was still there in his house packing, but—

Where was she going then?

How was he to know!

He was just letting her stay on? as she pleased?

But when he growled now what difference did it make to him or anybody how long she dilatorily dallied, *he* had her out of his hair hadn't he? Mrs. Barclay lightly made known her sheer incuriosity, he could tell her everything tomorrow if he insisted, when for fifteen minutes she would have one rushed cocktail with him at

Veale's, oh what did he merely *look* like again? for she could hardly wait to see!

And so, lingeringly, and (merely think!) till so soon, till almost in fact subito, she softly said their rivedersi; and hung up.

He sat beaming at the phone.

One moderately responsible woman left to him anyhow!

And went on beaming even when, having presently rung up Melissa for no real reason, he heard her phone sound on and on in an empty room and no one answered.

⋙§⋘

Under the dazzling country-summer morning, on a hill-top bowling-green set about thick with yews, Melissa's hostess and Melissa lolled by the plinth of a stone sundial and dried their hair, brushing brushing brushing, stylized little bodies ivory and gold in the immense light; brushed like young madwomen as they idly animadverted upon love.

"—adultery. Though who cares? Only Sam argues so!" the hostess was at that point complaining, of her husband, whose shorts, inside out, she was kneeling naked up in.

"Well she's insane, or d'you mean," yawned Melissa, naked too except for her own husband's, seam-out also.

"Well *admittedly* Liss, when she came right out of the grove with this boy!"

"Mm."

"In front of everybody!"

"Though even if nothing, you mean."

"Yes, after all *that* time!"

Melissa murmured "ouch, ow" to her brush, in languor. Her hostess fussed on, "Every touseled inch of her of course *looking* it."

"Mm."

"Why, it's just mindless of her!"

"Yes, when *any* husband would—"

"Lissa *love*, as if she cared!"

"But dear, even not; I mean one can just hear one's mothers on how irresponsible."

"Oh but that's Sam's interminable point, oh how stuffy Melissa you are!" wailed her best friend in muffled tones, head bowed in her silky tent, brush wildly fluffing and flying.

Melissa however, her short curls dry, had risen; she was posturing absently and languishingly, as in dance. "Why of course, poor love, oh darling mmm," she agreed, humming something.

"Oh where isn't it *dry* Liss, can you see?"

"What, dearest?" she vaguely sang, this young woman having been her roommate, at one time.

"Where not *dry*."

"*Not* dry?"

"Here?"

"Where?"

"Here!"

Melissa crooned, "Where, *here*?" approaching to touch deftly the cascading gold.

"And all in under."

"Well, no, not."

"Oh Lissa *hell*!"

"*Still* wants brushed," pronounced her guest in their private bogus Pennsylvania Dutch.

"Because husbands, what a creature they are," the hostess chafed, brushing in mad anguish once more. "Because I mean everybody always calls everybody else irresponsible when who knows what it is, responsibility I mean, well goodness!"

"Mmm."

"So unfair!"

"Oh darling men," Melissa sang, "darling darling men," turning in idle dance about the dial, sleek arms tenderly flailing.

"No but such *agony*, because Liss what would he do if *I*, I mean for pure hypothesis for example, what would Sam I mean, if I went to bed with somebody just melting and I couldn't help it, oh it's all so risky and unpredictable!" she whimpered.

"Dear, mm."

"No, but they're so *arbitrary*, when you think!"

Now gravely revolving in gavotte, Melissa intoned a dreamy "so anulnerous" in adenoidal.

"Oh of course who wouldn't be endlessly faithful to the great thing like a swooning thing," Sam's young wife fretted, brushing and brushing, "even married two everlasting years to him! Or anyhow nearly two; forever. Though Lissa?"

That one, however, wordlessly singing, turned and turned in the blissful day.

"Assuming merely. *Lissa!*"

"Mm?"

"Now admittedly *she* was mindless, if only fancy having herself caught like that, why as we said she *is* mad! but Liss if one were just this once on the whole *utterly* fetched, I mean by someone so—I mean what else is there but love one ever really thinks of!"

"So fond, so sad."

"Like Patrick for an example or someone madly sweetie like that, I mean d'you think? I mean for an *opinion* Lissa."

"Oh though look at them!" Melissa commanded, pirouetting to peer through the wall of yews down the green country slope at their two huge young husbands toiling in the stream-bed far below, in a thousand-fold flashing tesselation of aspens.

"No but *Lissa!*" her dearest friend agonized.

"How can they, oh how infantile!"

"Well they're delirious then," the hostess agreed in sheer distraction, coming up still brushing to peer too.

"How do men survive."

"Yes, when did *we* last build dams!"

"Will you merely *look*!"

"*Paddling in water!*"

They uttered little melodious screams.

"Wading!"

"When we were seven perhaps?"

"One's sweet little muddy panties sopping!"

So, swaying, hilarious, white and gold, these glossy little beauties clutched each other in helplessness, hooting at indecorous memories.

"Having in mere desperation to play half the summer with any little monster available!"

"Or mummy inviting those perfect little *rapists* from that great mouldering place beyond, so irresponsible!"

They drifted away. "Ah but Lissa think," her friend besought sadly, crouched drooping by the sundial once more, hair swaying down and aside as she brushed lovingly, indolently, on, "as to 'faithful' Liss I mean."

Melissa twisted her pretty torso in the blaze of noon, to see whether both little rocking breasts would cast their shadows, murmuring in agreement, "Hm? oh, *mm.*"

"No but *listen,*" the hostess said in her most careless tone, "because in her case it's admitted the boy wasn't married and all maddeningly involved already, but suppose he is, *both* sides of an affair I mean, assuming one were in love with some man who is. Was."

"Mm."

"Patrick as you suggested, for an example."

"What, love? who?" Melissa dreamed, a dying swan.

"*If you'd only listen!*" her roommate shrieked.

"Dearest, Patrick's married."

"*Yes*! and so what would that horrible little wife of his *do*, I mean, leave him for example or what? or might he even leave her or d'you think," she mused dreamily on, sweet head leaned aside.

"Well about *daddy* I certainly never thought!" Melissa cried out, standing still in shock.

"No but Liss, Patrick told me once that he—"

"Or about mummy leaving him! Well, I was beside myself, just *beside* myself!" she declaimed.

"Oh my arm is *dead*!" her hostess at once moaned, piteously writhing.

"I mean fancy mummy having so much spirit!"

"Dearest *could* you brush? if only till my arm—"

"Why *dearest*!" soothed her guest, "why *here*! But leaving daddy, of all possible men to want to leave! No bend *more*," she commanded the swaying gold, beginning to brush in gently sweeping parabolas.

"Yes you said."

"Because he isn't just anyone!"

"Oh terribly sweetie, why I adore him," the roommate absently agreed, twisting her little head half off to see down her pretty back.

"*Hold still!*" shrieked Melissa.

"No but I mean Liss—"

"Dearest you do have it long, you're mad."

"But when they want it long, because what can one do with them really, one *is* helpless Lissa."

"Ptah, not compared."

"Oh how can you, when I mean here we are responsible for men when it isn't even as if we were *responsible* for them!"

"Bend *over.*"

"Thhhhfffff," fuffed the friend, little scarlet mouth now full of gold.

"Of course mummy has no idea how to handle him."

"But when one can never quite be sure what they may do! Though what can one do in any case, Liss, ah, just drenched and drunk with a man the way one gets."

"There. Dry."

"Even when you *know* how they can be!"

"Mm."

"*So* irresponsible about us!"

"Ah, well," Melissa mourned, gazing down the slope once more at their pond-building husbands, gleaming among the aspens far below.

"Ah, they're *stones*, Liss," the hostess said.

As by the dark yews they clung together, slackly, in woe.

"Mad."

"This pool."

"This hysterical pool *exactly* and banking banking banking banking and who is it thinks up all the perversions."

So down they gazed in the enormous light, limply clinging, gazed and gazed, white and gold against the somber yews; swaying; spent.

" ... but they're *huge*," the glinting little hostess whispered presently, as in nameless dread.

They gaped at their great earth-moving animals, aghast.

Or dazed, in dream.

"This light," one murmured, in ultimate languor at last, breaking listlessly away.

"Dry now."

"Dry."

"Even long, dry."

"Even long, ah why does he," Melissa's hostess grieved, of whatever he, and drifted now finally across the clipped green and on, in, toward the vast cool glass livingroom beyond.

But Melissa, glittering indolently after her in the towering light, uttered only an indecipherable cry.

Mrs. Barclay being as it turned out late and Nicholas early, or as early anyway as a man in his right mind waiting for a pretty woman, he'd sat damn' near twenty minutes in Veale's unrecognizable bar, bolt-upright and presently glaring, before with a ripple of high heels in fluttered his angel in this breathless rush at last, blissfully gasping "Oh Nicholas oh simply now imagine!" as he lunged up from the banquette with a happy bellow to grab her—though this act she parried, after one radiant flash of blue eyes, by seizing and tenderly pressing his hands while uttering little winded cries of salutation and reminiscence; and having let him merely peck at one heavenly cheek eeled out of his arms to the seat, onto which she at once sank, blown.

"Now by heaven I was half-certain you weren't coming!" he cried out scrambling after her.

"............!" she panted wordlessly, batting those great eyes at him under a propitiatory hat-brim.

"When my god Victoria what an unearthly stylish lovely thing you are!"

"You're looking so *well*, Nicholas!" she replied to this.

"You've even got the sort of hat on by heaven you know makes me light-headed at the mere sight of you!"

"—and so beautifully turned out, really when can anyone have seen you looking so handsome," she ran on, flinging a spring fur neatly between them and scattering gloves and handbag about her in practiced piles.

He rumbled, "Now, an unbolted old wreck actually," much pleased.

"So tall, so imperial, *fancy* forgetting, oh why simply look at you, now you must tell me instantly how you've been Nicholas, how *are* you, oh I could lose my heart to you all over again from sheer good manners!" she cried lightly. Immediately adding, "Actually of course I bought it weeks ago," of the hat.

Adrift at this, he said, "Did, huh," signalling the waiter.

"*Long* before you rang up!"

"Unh? first person I called!"

"So you see quite plainly, even if it did, or does, happen to be your sort!"

"Now my lovely Victoria what's this now?" he demanded competently, eye on a waiter charging headlong.

"Well Nicholas *who* in her right mind! when you know as well as I do we hadn't thought of each other for d— for years," the lovely untrustworthy thing assured him, tilting down her hat-brim momentarily as a shield against the only polite answer anybody could make to this, viz., that it was a damn' lie.

The waiter here plunged up trundling a champagne-cooler asplash with frost. A heavy captain followed, and now with his thick thumbs grasped the cork, breathing through his mouth fussily. So while the fellow lengthily poured, Nicholas groaned, "Drinks with you again my utter blessed woman my god imagine it!" in the stricken accents of idolatry.

They drank. She murmured in tones of happiest misgiving, blue eyes for one melting instant deep in his, that he knew she had in twelve minutes quite literally to fly.

"Now my sweet Victoria you can't intend to go *on* like this dammit!" he burst out, "in the manner of that icy salutation? Giving me a *cheek* to kiss my god!"

At this she had the sensibility to cast her eyes down, sipping.

"Ah, that lovely mouth, color of pink dogwood," he droned along, as in most moving elegy, "and then to treat me in that absol— "

"After seventeen years?" she cried at him. "*Oh* how unfair!"

" 'Unfair'!"

"And *upsetting* then to be meeting you again Nicholas! If you'd even thought about me enough to *see* how I must feel!"

"But my sweetest angel—"

"Am I then to dash forgivingly here there and everywhere falling into the arms of strangers in any bar they happen to name?"

" '*Strangers*'!" he bayed.

"And now you yell at me!" she breathed, absolutely shutting her pretty eyes.

So it seemed time for him to say, beginning to laugh, "Not yell, why how can I converse then?"

She pouted, sipping.

"Well, can I?"

"Oh you *wound* me so, Nicholas!" she announced through the rim of her glass, which she now drained. And as he refilled it, "When seeing you is such a—   When merely meeting you again like this is—is so—"

"I just want to point out my restraint, my decorum!" he cried.

"And you *know* we have to be!"

"My blessed Victoria—"

"We do we *do*!" she wailed.

Here the captain loomed over them again, heavy jaw civilly ajar, to turn the bottle in its floes.

The moment however the fellow got around to taking himself off, Nicholas declared she *knew* he'd for days done nothing but think about her in the most heart-shaking terms; with the most eager, the most affecting anticipation; 'd hardly slept, anticipating; and now here she took it into her heavenly head to drive him distracted with expressions like "decorum"! and in a word what sin was she pleased to assign him in the room of adoring her? he ended in his most bravura Restoration manner, draining off his glass with a smack of his lips and picking up her furs from between them to deposit the damn' things out of the way. But by this time that mouth-breather stood over them again pouring; now, sucking his thick tongue, he uttered judgements concerning this blanc de blancs, which he described as "Heidsieck." So they had to sit while for some time this went on.

Mrs. Barclay then at once lightly veered and began prying delicately into his divorce: how did he feel about it then, so tedious for him, she told him in well-groomed tones and gave him little shuttered glances, so distressing and putting-out of his wife, how could she!

He pronounced it in his view an insult of a not very refined sort.

"She's in love?"

"Now what's this," he growled.

"Well but she must be you mean naturally," Mrs. Barclay urged, fixing him with great watchful eyes.

"My wife?"

"Or in love with somebody you don't know?"

"Why should she be dammit, no!"

"But nobody at *all*?" the charming thing cried as if distracted.

"Ah, well, possibly some insulting second marriage soon enough, I make no doubt!" he snarled, conceding. "Ought to wring her pretty neck now, for all I know; save her from some subsequent god's-own folly. How's anyone to say what'll take your babbling undiscriminating bewildered hearts next!" he ended in exasperation, and poured again, drizzling.

"But Nicholas my dear didn't she say?"

"Say what? My point is—"

"But Nicholas she—"

"Point I'm trying to make dammit," he insisted, "is, here she was for years, a most delicious sweet creature actually, I suppose; for *years*, Victoria! Yet now this happens, and abruptly I find I have to ask myself after all was she," he said in dejection, draining off his glass.

Mrs. Barclay let fall into hers, "in love, how sad," sipping.

"Well then," he rumbled, deeply cast down.

"But *you* now, poor darling," she said in instant encouragement, "what have you in mind then, your *plans* Nicholas I mean," she urged him, sipping several little mouthfuls more, of which she absently sighed, " ... delicious."

And as he said nothing, "No but your coming *here* I meant," she gently probed, and pushed her glass for him to refill yet again.

He appeared to think, pouring. "Urban type, why not," he offered, morosely.

"Because don't you remember your own epigram about New York all that time ago, is why," she explained, and drank. "Ah Nicholas *so* delicious again!" she admitted, of whatever, smiling over the glass's rim into his eyes. "Spilling it, oh darling shaming," she mumbled happily, having slopped.

"Epigram, huh."

"What, darling?"

"This epigram about New York you claim I made."

"Yes you said New York was a terrible place but other places were *terrible* places."

"By god now did I?" he said, delighted.

"You found it terribly funny," she murmured, little nose dreamily in her glass once more.

"And you remembered it, my angel!"

"Well you kept using it for weeks; so sweet, oh Nicholas."

"But anyhow naturally I came here, d'you maintain you've had for one seraphic second to wrack your brain wondering why?"

"Ah Nicholas."

"My sweetest Victoria as if you didn't—"

"I *never* think about you!" she cried out tearfully.

"Now you're not pretending you hadn't even thought about me coming here to meet me!"

"Oh what mad egotism! while I was *shopping*?"

"Well so then you did though!"

"Well how childish, well of course why wouldn't I or anybody?" she told him crossly.

"And made this unnerving decision to manoeuvre me into merely kissing your cheek by heaven!"

" 'Decide,' " she quoted with heat, " 'decide,' as if one 'decided' on the only natural normal— *Nicholas*!" she hissed in sudden outrage, for the waiter had swooped in rolling a second wine-cooler to set beside the first, the captain following with his catarrh to twist out the cork and meatily pour.

At this piece of foresight, the moment they withdrew Mrs. Barclay organized a scene. "Your preparations!" she blazed.

"Of course now the fellow's an imbecile dammit! All I—

"*Two bottles*! as if I were—"

"Now Victoria it simply struck me, 'd strike anybody, one bottle's a mere couple of glasses."

"Oh what an utter staring lie, a sheer dozen!"

"Two glasses apiece at the outs— "

"A *dozen*!" she as good as screamed at him. "Call back that smirking waiter and see then!" she commanded smouldering, "oh how can you be so carelessly unfeeling to me!"

" 'Careless'!" he cried, in tones of one reeling.

"So impervious to how you upset me, *ask* him how many glasses in a bottle, ask that snuffling ox of a captain, oh how selfish you are!" she rebuked him, draining off her glass.

So he had to summon the man back.

"Now Mr. Romney's agreed you shall settle a bet for us," she cooed at him, explaining what—the fellow wheezing, "ah, precise, madam, aha," and the like.

"Simply how many glasses in a bottle d'you figure on normally then," Nicholas demanded.

"Is a metter call for a nize judgment, sair."

"I mean by and large dammit."

"A tremendous number, I'm persuaded," Mrs. Barclay serenely proclaimed.

"Allows a mostly seven, Madam."

"You see?" she crowed happily at Nicholas.

"I said there weren't anything like a doz— "

"You said four, *four*, whereas this man who has to pour cases and cases every day in mere line of duty said seven as you heard as a minimum," she explained to him in tones of charm.

"If you call a three-ounce restaurant glass—"

"I suppose you'll pretend to me you'd think nothing of draining off four three-ounce glasses of Martinis then!"

He shouted, "Now by god you know I won't have a Martini in the house! As seventeen years ago you were perfectly well aware!"

"You not only yell at me," she at once charged in a low quivering voice, "and are as unkind and purposely intransigent as you know how but you pretend I've forgotten your stuffy prejudiced habits too!"

On this he instantly pounced. "And so you *have* forgotten, and boast of it!" he happily proclaimed.

Mrs. Barclay, not having quite seen this coming, sat with her lovely mouth ajar.

"Heartlessly and unfeelingly forgotten!" he ran on, eyes alight, "whereas not one single thing you ever did with me has left my mind for a day, not one sweet word you ever said, Victoria, not a day or night I swear to you in all this endless gloom of time!''

She glared in miserable silence.

''Why, you've even forgotten what you swore that last night at— *Have* you forgotten?''

''I won't tell you,'' she sniffled, nose in her glass.

''When I'd waited half that afternoon in the Via del Babuino—''

''I didn't mean to make you wait!'' she cried in remorse.

''You came racing toward me through the traffic, every man in sight staring his heart out at the mere lovely glimpse of you!''

''You were teaching me to drink those horrible Roman drinks. And now you bring me here and abuse me about champagne,'' she accused him in melting tones, sadly draining her glass.

''My lovely Victoria, as if you didn't know I'm as wild over you this minute, no matter what damn' wrangle, as I was the last instant I had you in my arms.''

(Which phrase simultaneously and at once recalled to them that this had occurred, to specify, in a huge Roman cinquecento bedroom, early in a summer dawn, in a bed littered with the fragrant though by then ruined petals of three or four dozen gardenias.)

'' ... so spoiled, such an actual child,'' she said dolefully.

'' 'Spoiled'! when your very kiss of greeting—''

''When I indulge you so, ah when I do everything you want and I shouldn't; why here I am *meeting* you!''

''And you never meet anybody for a drink? you lovely transparent— Just meeting me for a simple drink you feel adulterous, do you, you heavenly thing!'' he told her, in rapture, pouring once more.

''*Nicholas!*''

''Then by god what did that angel's remark mean?''

''I won't tell you!''

''You sweet guilty—''

''Oh how *irresponsible* you are!'' she screamed at him, pink with exasperation.

And so on and so on. As they went on down into the second cool delicious bottle.

The conversation becoming still less worth setting even ceremonially down.

⋘⸙⸙⋙

So next morning she had to ring him up in bland complaisance to
have him know it had been so agreeable to see him that could he
imagine what she'd forgotten to tell him? the one thing she'd meant
to say to him, too! it had just skidded out of her mind utterly, she
urbanely informed him, and it had been almost her main reason for
meeting him as she had, only fancy!

Viz., why couldn't she lend him a man for his little Barrow Street
house if that was where he was going to be for a time—look after
him, or till he'd hired one for himself, this man happening she said
to serve as chef on her chef's days out though bred for a valet, so it
took care of everything. For why for one unlikely moment think
that he (Nicholas) could put up with staying at Veale's when as he
well knew hotels just upset him, they had ways of doing things he
wasn't used to and he had tantrums, even at Veale's, so she wanted
to lend him this *excellent* man. So then he could move in practically
at once then, did he see? into his charming small empty house in
Barrow Street as soon as he pleased, with its little oval Adam stair
and she remembered *tiny* elegant low-ceiling'd rooms, fancy a
Philadelphia family's having these eighteenth-century properties in
New York, how unexpected.

(There being however nothing remarkable about this—a great-
grandmother of Nicholas's had simply been this New York heiress
et voilà—what Mrs. Barclay presumably meant instead was that she
forbade all mention of a folly she now so wholly repented of that
she did not even remember it, namely how she'd made love with
him in nearly every room in the place at one time and another,
even, as he well knew also, on the elegant stair.)

So, he could shortly move in; and did.

To find nothing changed, moreover everything in good condi-
tion, though by some madness of apparently Melissa's (who'd lived
there the first year she was married) the Copley ancestor over the
fireplace in the front drawing-room had been lugged off to the
garret and in its place there hung, of all possible portraits, that
damn' painter's Early Prospect Of Mrs. Hume or whatever title

he'd assigned it. So this had to be carried up to the garret and the Copley fetched down again and hung.

And he himself unpacked (while Victoria's man was unpacking him) a manila folder of assorted private relics, which he stowed one by one in the upstairs scrutoire—an engraved *William and Priscilla Neave desire thy presence at the wedding of* a girl who in due course became his mother; an old New Year's card written out in a college roommate's easy scrawl "with every warmest platitude of the season"

> Well, Nick boy? Both of us alive,
> Another year receipted.
> Here's luck—in 1955,
> Almighty God, we'll need it!

—kept not for luck, God knows, the poor devil having been shot dead in Walnut Street hardly a month after writing the thing, by some crazed Camden shipwright who mistook him for somebody he thought was keeping his daughter, never really cleared up who; an enlarged snapshot of two baby boys and two sub-adolescent girls (Melissa mugging) with a dog named Dirdy Giotto, now dead; and then suddenly here was his tall charming young wife years ago, her eyes looking lovingly straight at him, faintly smiling. So he stared at this for some time.

Still, when presently he went down to where in the back drawing-room that gave on the garden the man had the evening champagne iced and ready and an evening tabloid in (headlined *Sex Shill Czar Probe Fix Hit*) and sat sipping till dinner, musing on Victoria he felt better, in fact went down to dinner murmuring be damned if for all he could tell he'd been relieved of the endearing fatigues of one of the sweet creatures only to have the vaporings of another imposed.

For the place was how agreeably haunted again! and after dinner he rang her up to move her by telling her so, meaning also to report that the guinea-with-gin she'd had her man serve him (now imagine her remembering of all his dishes that one!) had been admirably cooked, he'd had a Clos de Vougeot with it, and then the fellow's poires dorées, cool and fragrant and all the more so from *her* having ordered it all for him, she was as womanly sweet as she was sexually delicious did she know that? so he'd taken his coffee and marc out into the little brick-walled garden in this early-June night so full of her *and* her dinner that he could hardly wait to hear her angelic accents over the wire.

Except when some confounded domestic answered by god she wasn't even in!

Nor what's more had left word when she might be!

So will you credit it? he had to put in the evening planning his house-warming himself, lists lists lists, endless goddam roster of his friends, names and faces and matching them up and with not even secretarial womanly help sorting out memory.

So, he borrowed a couple of Victoria's maids too and asked enough people after these twenty years to pack his little house to the walls, couldn't have been more agreeably nostalgic, might have been the Thirties all over again, rooms jammed and milling, uproar deafening, guests in no time overflowing in clamoring waves out over the flagstones and turf of the garden and down into the little dining-room, sitting gabbling on the stairs, even racketing up into the bedroom and the writing-room behind it—bankers brokers New York classmates amiably baying at him across the din in welcoming and heart-warming quantity, wives offering a cheek to his kiss, a few even putting up a smiling mouth in undeceived reminiscence, even the usual number of people he damn' well disliked; also his lawyer up from Philadelphia with his bulging brief-case, the sheer tax-manoeuvring his wife's behavior had now got him into! his own cursing yeoman forebears hadn't been amerced with a blacker set of reliefs and merchets, church-scot and plough-alms and smoke-farthings and hearthpenny on Holy Thursday, and nowadays who could he tallage in return? and of course Melissa.

Who fled in darting glances of piercing young appraisal at everything as she proclaimed, "Sweetie, champaginny and all, well how *coo*," absently presenting her angel cheek.

Which he kissed, grumbling happily, "Now what's this, afraid I'll muss you dammit?"

"Well *daddy*."

"Tirée à quatre épingles like that," he beamed.

But she cried, "Why, you've changed everything, now who's *that*?" of the Copley ancestor; though what difference who? she hadn't had a notion who Angelina's portrait had been of either.

Also several New York nieces and nephews he had recalled he had and a young cousin or two. And to keep that generation at least amused he'd told Melissa ask some of her friends if she liked, why not (husband too of course if the fellow could forget his bank long enough); also Victoria had her stepson, son of her husband by a first marriage, name of Toby or something of the sort, who it appeared might well bring a girl he was in a daze at (a little actress, rather sweet and mad, Victoria said). So in a word he'd asked pretty much everybody, even children. Though not his sons, they having final exams.

Everybody crying out with indulgent urbanity how wonderful again, how well he looked and what a jewelbox of a little house lost way down here, how had they ever forgotten how it enchanted them, this small elegant eighteenth-century house he had, these tiny charming rooms, this heavenly stair, bawling at him across the commemorating pandemonium how particularly fine *now* when everyone was pulling down everything everywhere, demolishing demolishing, the Brevoort rubble the Meadowbrook a scavo, why was there nothing anyone could do? though they demanded what could anyone *do*! when if wishes were horses (had he heard this one?) if wishes were horses we'd have a population of centaurs.

Also what were his plans, as a corollary would he perhaps now live way down here? this part of the Village having after all, since the Thirties, changed.

So it took time before he got in two words edgewise with his Victoria by backing her for a happy moment into the curve of the piano, on which some drunken couple he'd never seen in his life were accompanying themselves in what sounded like

Se amor non è, che dunque è quel ch'io sento

—this-can't-be-love but probably turn out to be Petrarch he roared in her ear and he *loved* her, would she for once get it through her stylish head how he adored her? because *god* what a lovely thing she was and why in His bellowing name had he ever invited these crashing intruding people that kept her from walking into his arms that instant, for had she any notion how frightful it was? because how could she!

She however as if conducting this at some undisingenuous pace had already begun to tell him she'd been thinking about what he'd not really said, had he; of their conversation the other day, she meant; she meant at Veale's.

He said said what.

Couldn't he pay even passing attention? said *why*. This divorce she wanted; why she wanted it; his wife. After all these years why of all moments this one!

Did he have to keep saying and then saying again? she had not said! Which was one reason that final infamous interview—

But surely no matter what he might evasively or even guiltily say in denial he must nevertheless know! She must have had some reason, possibly some very *good* reason, oh what had he contrived to spill on his waistcoat now? she cried in pique, scrubbing at it, or was the hideous truth (which he dared not admit to her) simply that he'd made love to one other woman more than his wife's nerves could finally stand! she finished in a passion.

But as he was about to reply in amazed innocence the drunks from the piano-bench joined them. So then they all had to converse in halting Italian for some minutes, the man of this couple turning out to the universal surprise to be a classmate who'd roomed in the same entry of '79 Hall.

Until some courtly ox joined them proclaiming (in English) what a hell of a fine little house this was, had he lived here all these years by god? made him think of what's-his-name's over in East 10th, astonishing how similar, what *was* the poor devil's name, knew it as well as he knew his own, everybody knew him, knew about him anyhow, used to rent a handsome baby to wheel round Washington Square as a conversation-starter, they remember? used to say he was its uncle! Or its grandfather, depended on how he assessed the temperament of whatever pretty little piece he was engaged in picking up; *dead* now, of a thundering heart-attack not six months before, poor charming lecherous old devil, 'change and decay on ev'ry hand descry,' however it went whatever it was; who'd expect the law of averages applied to the upper classes!

After this threnody he and the drunken Petrarchians rambled off. Nicholas instantly resumed, demanding of Mrs. Barclay with amazed innocence other women other women must she like a pervicacious angel think that because he loved her with every beat of his heart, loved and had loved, as she herself well remembered and in this house should remember best of all—

Mrs. Barclay regretted seeing that he still had the discreditable habit of avoiding a review of his conduct by reminding her of flaws in her own! because she had simply been *very young* then, then when she'd loved him, young and as he was well aware infatuated, what did one know of one's emotional responsibilities at that age? what *could* one know!

He said but—

And what arguments could *he* marshal of innocence and youth, then or now, what pretext of a heart's sweet first love, in the sheer rake's progress of his protestations! she cried at him through the hubbub around them, driving his wife too she had no doubt at long-suffering last to such despair!

But as he was replying with tenderest raillery now what ever gave woman the notion that she was monogamous, here came a ponderous old dandy to kiss Mrs. Barclay's hand, describing to her what a happy assault on his peace of mind the mere sight of her was! thank God the convulsing of man's equanimity still constituted female comportment, and then in turn describing to Nicholas how damn' heartening to see a man in his own establishment for once, would he conceive the Club nowadays couldn't even set out a routine breakfast? porridge thin and they pretended they'd never heard of Demarara sugar, the buttered eggs weren't buttered but *scrambled* in God's name! a catalogue of barbarism he'd not offend Mrs. Barclay's lovely ear by reciting further. Would they tell him what had become of the ordinary decencies? with nothing left but a new outrage daily to add to the series of indignant bellows with which thank God he still greeted reality!

So Nicholas had to say yes by god take an ordinary interest in what food one ate and what resulted? his own children denominated him a pig! and Victoria said snappishly there at *last* was her never-on-time young mountain of a stepson, had he never met Nicholas's Melissa? because she must see he did instantly! and was off.

So the old boy demanded of Nicholas who were all these children? by god they baffled him, this generation, they appeared to think sex was a branch of psychotherapy. Now his and Nicholas's generation—well, take a leathery cousin of his own who when divorced had set up this showgirl in a little flat, perfectly normal showgirl, tendency to go to bed with outfielders; but all the same—

Here however a huge handsome white-haired classmate flung himself jovially upon them, one great ape's arm round each, to beg in a whooping and waggish stage-whisper don't stop him *now* goddammit, his ear had just this moment picked up across the din a sound it had been delightedly attuned to catching lo these many years, the hunting-cry of a pretty woman who'd suddenly realized how *much* her damn' husband bored her—the angel promise of which music he for one could hear over the braying of a party mob four times the size of this one and would they in God's happy name not delay him till some low lecher got to her first? so off he caromed in that direction. And Nicholas at once in another, it being high time he worked his way down to the kitchen to see to supplies.

So that was where he was, leaning against a counter and having this peripatetic extra glass of champagne to himself in momentary peace for once (nothing *against* his friends and contemporaries of course but they poured champagne down as if they took it for gin, by heaven)—the kitchen was where he was, pouring himself still another glass in fact, when speaking of the younger generation the door swung gently open and closed again, and in had stepped this beautiful child.

Who came softly up to him and stood smiling into his eyes as if she not just worshipped him but meekly owned him, and said in a voice like a lovely bell, "Ah, I knew I'd meet you again, some day somehow Nicholas, if I only waited and oh, so hoped."

And there he was, dazzled.

Mind utterly ajar.

"You don't even *remember* me!" she cried, instantly pink.

He managed to get out what on earth'd she mean? not remember, why good god!

"You don't remember my name even!" she upbraided him, a great topaze tear trembling in either eye. "Whereas *I* remember every time I was even in miles of West Chester!"

From some desperate mineshaft of recollection he came up with a what nonsense her name was Morgan, *Morgan*, and she'd permit him to add as pretty as a—

"Well when after all Nicholas I was at your house that whole weekend at your own daughter's house-party, I mean who could be so stupid," she demanded as if reasonably. "Though of course she says it's Melissa you pay all the attention to."

So thus he was able to assure her in heartiest tones why certainly! why, she'd been at some acting school or other over on the Main Line then hadn't she; or wait, she'd been about to play Ophelia in some off-Broadway art-loft at the time, anyhow Juliet perhaps or some equally star-crossed but unhelpless ingénue, he beamed.

"Well there was also something else that weekend you might be nice enough to me to remember too Nicholas if you weren't so puritanical and formal," she complained serenely, casting down her cycs. "Except I bet you don't even think I should call you by your first name even, do you! when what would you *expect* me to call you? when of course I always call you Nicholas to myself, how else could I even think about you!"

He started to remark, well, he imagined that if that obsolete noun punctilio were to be observed—

But she was murmuring with a sweet look at him, "I don't suppose it ever crosses your mind that I think about you even more than I think about myself, oh people are such *mysteries* to each other, Nicholas," she confided, while with his courtliest air he made to fill her glass. "No one ever suspects what I really think inside! Except once in one's life one can meet this one person one wants to know one's whole secret mystery—and I don't see why you won't just *admit* when it is you, my dearest!" she finished in a sudden little fury.

He gaped out a what?! now what on earth was she—

"Well, we women are simply *helpless* then sometimes in our

dealings with you, why can't you see!'' she fumed as if explaining, stamping her little foot. ''Oh but I forgive you anyhow though Nicholas,'' she went on happily, ''because after all that weekend, well of course I was just too young and inexperienced to work on you wasn't I, oh if I'd known then what I know now oh think what I could have made you do! It was a whole year ago, well I was simply young and *infatuated* if you insist on knowing.''

He said, looking at her pretty warily, now now now now, she wasn't forgetting the way her whole charming sex tended to operate, was she? and when all a man might be doing was his poor reeling best!

And before she could decipher this, he a bit too rapidly cantered on: why, just try persuading some heavenly creature you adored her, would she consent to listen accurately to the honest pounding of your heart? on the contrary she flounced and turned her back on you and pouted that you didn't *really* love her (mind you, the poor stricken devil expiring of love right there under her elegant little nose!) didn't really *love* her, you didn't you didn't you only wanted to get into bed with her and why was she ever born! yes, and before you could summon the wits to combat this heartless libel the lovely thing would moan, 'Because you *do* want to go to bed with me don't you?' and when you stammered out good-god-*yes*, what did she do but shriek '*You see?*' and burst into tears!

So she looked at him with shining eyes.

So then he more or less unavoidably had to pat her shoulder assuasively, smiling down.

After what may have been a long moment therefore the child drooped her lashes at him, softly saying, ''Well you ought to be able to *see*, Nicholas, that you're so darling to me so much of the time that when you're mean to me what could I be but furious.''

He said now now.

But she went on, lower still, ''Ah, couldn't you be kind enough to me just this once to admit you remember what you know did happen that weekend, any of it?'' And now not looking at him, in fact sinking against him sighing, she whispered as if, ah, undone, ''Even that one lovely kiss, my dearest?''

So what was the great gruff man to do?

—Except that almost before he could utter some croaked reply this sudden little suppliant of his was out of his arms again and standing there before him in instantaneous composure. As the door opened; and not unnaturally at all, there was Mrs. Barclay.

Who at once, or nearly at once, exclaimed in a wholesome voice, "So *here*'s where you are, my dear d'you know your young man's been hunting high and low for you this good half-hour? This child has bewitched my stepson, or can you wonder!" she cried at Nicholas. "Now Morgan dear you know how he gets to *be*, he goes along quite capably but then suddenly it comes to him he's hungry! so hadn't you better cope? The huge thing, he's a j.g. already, Nicholas, fancy! or did you even realize his mother was that sister of Angelina Hume's?—somebody I'm sorry to say Mr. Romney imagined he was particularly fetched by at one time," she explained in tones of womanly forbearance, to Morgan, smiling at these bygone foibles, for how immature.

So Morgan smoothly chatted, yes *poor* Toby, taking her to dinner when she'd told him what could she do but feed and imperatively *fly*? with studio rehearsals at the hour they were! even just when he had his first leave in so long. Whereupon in he lumbered beaming and bore his little actress away.

Mrs. Barclay at once said in a different tone altogether now please might she ask to have a drop more champagne in a glass he seemed unaware had been empty she had no notion how long, his attention having been elsewhere? in fact what exactly *had* he conceived he was doing all this time! Or did he even know? she demanded in disdain.

He said, stunned, 'doing'? she mean here? canvassing supplies in his own kitchen?

Oh how convenient it must be not to recognize criticism when he heard it! A man of his age! And when this hardly stable girl— Why, even if no other impediment, even if no early misconduct of his, marriage with Toby would make her Angelina's niece!

He stammered what? completely at sea.

She said violently what did he *mean* 'what'!!

Why, he begged her, was she suggesting— What *was* she suggesting?

He had the effrontery to pretend he didn't *know*?

But what possible implication of consanguinity— Even if it were possible it would be an *impossible* thing! when there hadn't been a shadow of— And in any case, why, dammit, the girl had no more than just come into the kitchen! the plain inhospitable fact being moreover that he hadn't known the little thing from Eve!

Then why was he kissing her in a kitchen!

He cried by god he'd done no such thing! this much being the simple truth anyhow.

Was he then saying in addition to every other slur that she lacked the most elementary powers of observation? Though what had she ever had from him but one mistruth after another! Or had he forgotten his ignoble epigram: 'a man lies to women because they won't know what to believe if he doesn't'! she quoted, pale with rage, and for all she knew he did have that affair with the unhappy boy's mother too!

He implored her—

In fact the *real* question was not whether Toby might be his own huge innocent son but whether she, Victoria, ought ever to speak to him again at all! she raved.

And fled the very sight of him.

— This, mind you, when he hadn't done one damn' thing! Had merely stood there! In ordinary civilized good manners! And the boy didn't in the least look like him anyway.

⋙⋘

Past all expectation, then, after the party, his rooms empty now and echoing, servants gone, he stalked through his deserted house pretty down in the mouth, pretty *glum* if you want a word! baring his teeth at that boiled mutton of a Copley, a goddam bleached Puritan and no conceivable ancestor for a man who liked pretty women.

Or stood, too, for a time, at one of the tall front windows staring in irresolution out into the luminous city night (how charged with memory); or again, drifted back once more, to touch the empty curve of the piano with his remembering hand.

And in this dim hallway too she had so often stood! this scrolled and gilded glass had held her image in its blackening depths; why, it was here she had fought him laughing that day he bought her the Hindu nose-jewel and pinioned her struggling and gently slipped it on (which with little salvoes of apologetic kisses she had at once slipped off, and never worn again); at this stair-foot too she had once stood weeping in his arms. And up the interlacing ovals of the stair, the half-landing with its clasped and happy ghosts (they'd all but rolled down), and so on up, in emptiness, in desolation, until here was the very room, the rosewood field-bed with its vased turnings, sheet laid smoothly back in its waiting triangle—*here*, where once he'd woken and found her, lapped in the first early warm-ivory light, hand held high in the dawn-rose shadows at the end of that Botticelli arm, staring as if unseeing at the dull gold of her husband's ring. So he stood at that room's windows too; looking out in *rebuke*, by heaven! growling despondently his Ovidian tag (hic fuit, hic cubuit, however the thing went); and so, out, finally, sighing, alone, into the unobliterating night.

For there too, as he wandered east along 10th Street, in which house had it been, between Sixth Avenue and Fifth? behind the French windows with their fine ironwork filigree, that he and a girl in a fluttery jonquil-colored summer dress, in the amiable din of an all-night party, or anyhow in the moonless garden behind—   But what had even been her name? and perhaps hadn't it happened over east of Fifth Avenue anyhow? at that advertising classmate's with a dyke of a wife?

—But in God's name *where was the Brevoort*? A hoarding screened the site; wreckers' hooded and implacable engines lay moored at the nighted curb.

Pulling it down! *Gone!*

In the violet air the gutted brick cellars gaped, the roofless walls reeled and fell ("Pompeii!" he cried hollowly aloud) amid a litter of stucco-duro medallions and tumbled capstones, the sprawling plinths of rubble in an ordered Palatine desolation. "And to make room for *what* supererogatory forty-storey glass slum," he said at last, turning heavily (and now, forever) away: terrasse dark, sidewalk tables gone, an outrage, an ultimate outrage, not just to him but to a whole geography of human recollection, memories by the tens of thousands, of honorable established people who wanted a gleaming properly laid table and good food well served and some delicious creature or other to have dinner with on a fine early-summer evening as the lights came on in the baldachin of dusk and the nightfall murmur of traffic died slowly away uptown along the Avenue and down into Washington Square, this very Brevoort moreover where he and his Victoria had met for lunch that first fatal and enchanted rendezvous, the mere second time they'd ever laid eyes on each other, ah God what a prelude to what an afternoon and a lifetime! her poise the glossiest finishing-school cloisonné as he paid off her taxi but her eyes overflowing with light at him before she'd even sipped her vermouth cassis, full of happy terror by the entree and ah, by dessert hardly able to look at him, the lovely undefended undefendable angel! and God knows he himself hardly able to breathe! in the sunlit delirium of youth both of them, shaken and dizzy at the sheer miracle of each other—until at last over their brandy her eyes opening to him radiant and amorous, and as if she would never look away from him again.

And now that tender ghost vanished; lost; the toppling wreckage untenanted and menacing before him; and here ahead (in the most piteous possible phrasing) stretched out empty the long night-reaches of the soul.

So he stumped home to bed.

Homesick for his woods too by heaven, in this impalpable night; his ancient beeches, or in his parks of oak the wild azalea now, the dogwood, still in flower; and up the darkening lawns of that irrecoverable past his silly charming children scampering shrieking; lost they too; done with him; gone. So he poured himself a marc in lieu of nightcap and the hell with what it did to his liver, and went moodily to bed.

Where he then lay tossing in the dark, snarling.

For what could anybody maintain he'd done to this unaccountable wife of his? when he'd done nothing! *Literally* nothing and what fault might be lay at her door not his!

Or if change his character, what change? Moreover what change could she or anybody expect of a man of fifty? Or as good as.

How did a lifetime of decent-minded experience prepare a man for being flat deserted? And why *now*? for what was he the day she'd coldly said good-bye to him that he hadn't been every day for decades, what had he done? Or not done? Or had a man's behavior toward woman anything at all to do, finally, with whether she fluttered into his astounded arms or, conversely, out of them.

So he flumped, sleepless.

All these years and then suddenly a woman not there any more! Years of the most conspicuous and patient Responsibility, too, if that was the argument! And admittedly a man who liked women had to put up with being responsible about them in some degree. Though responsible responsible, in what sense responsible goddammit? aside from treating them with a cushiony consideration.

"And how's anybody know!" he burst out at last, snapping on the bedside light, glaring, "with mankind for all I can tell not responsible just involved—hopeless from start to finish," he railed, and flung on his dressing-gown. "What if there's no fault then, tell me that, none on either side, hers or mine, poor creature, poor sweet creature, what then? with for all I know all love a flow, a flux, a phase, an end," he droned dispiritedly and rhetorically on, shuffling out and to the stair.

And muttering "—talking to myself like a goddam great-aunt" padded down for another marc.

Which might have put him to sleep except that at two in the morning his Senior son rang him up.

He roared in utter affront, "Now God *damn* it Nickie you aware what *hour* this is?!"

" ..... "

"You *what*?"

" ..... "

"What's that hellish racket, where the deafening hell are you anyway!"

" ..... "

"Some fetid dive in short!"

" ..... "

"*Damn* what the swine play, foul dive like any other!"

" ..... "

"In any case I was given to understand you were off at Poughkeepsie, what the devil are you rutting around after some mincing girl for when as I understood it by god haven't you got exams?"

"....."

"*Told* me you were in Poughkeepsie."

"....."

"One of that stampeding horde you room with, how do I know which?"

"....."

"Oh but *she* had an exam! now how damn' insensible of her! in a word though you had to *go* all the way to Poughkeepsie to discover they give exams at this time of the year too?"

"....."

"Yes but if you don't have her with you why in God's nightlong name aren't you down at Princeton studying yourself?"

"....."

"*Who* instead?"

"....."

"How do I know their names, describe her. Is this that stylish little Goucher—"

"....."

"Had an exam *too*, yes I do see! So with the most fertile masculine resourcefulness you've conjured up still a third young woman to share this pandemonium you're phoning from."

"....."

"Well, 'fourth' then; a fourth."

"....."

"But in the medieval monastic phrase how many of these little angels do you conceive you're balancing on the point of a needle simultaneously?"

"....."

"I said, how many damn' girls are you responsible for at the moment, what d'ye think I said!"

"....."

"Well, *ir*responsible for then. Involved with."

"....."

"No but I mean it's all very well to collect young women in this flattering quantity, even in variety Nickie, couldn't *be* a more fashionable pastime I know and I do sympathize, if not a rake why else born? undergraduate myself once let me remind you! And heaven defend us from a mere parochial taste in women anyhow. Nevertheless, Nickie, has it, uh, never struck you—"

"....."

"Well *obviously* my dear boy they're there to be made love to within selected limits but you can't have the Boeotian insensibility to imagine that that's all!"

"....."

"A limit I naturally mean to the extent a man feels free to bemuse what may in fact be a, huh, be a very tender and uncertain little heart dammit!"

"....."

"Now don't talk like a *child* Nickie!"

"....."

"Look here dammit just *correct* this attitude of yours a little in the direction of reason and good manners will you! I don't propose to be rung up at three in the morning to be instructed in the defects of my judgment, fondness for you or no fondness!"

And hung *up*, by god! And sat fuming.

Presently, yawning, he went down to the kitchen in the back basement and rummaged in sheer parental exasperation in the icebox and sliced a few slivers from a ham. With four eggs in a little parsley omelette he made to go with it. Also a bowl of porridge the man had quite properly made overnight in advance. Sampled a couple of jars of jam, too, on some left-over croissants; and a peach and a slice of melon, the melon not very good so he got rid of the taste with two more peaches. Last him anyhow till breakfast.

The day after this, Melissa and Melissa's dearest friend met uptown at their charity, doing thankless Lists.

Hours long, a soft gabble, musing, as in Arcadia, choral turn and turn.

Melissa chanting, "—this simple black Moygashell-linen sheath with horizontal tucking at the yoke with I think a box jacket though she had it over her arm so who could tell? with that Aztec-ish embroidery, and the *hat* one of those little cones of straw and lattice veiling, so how would you decide?" of Mrs. Barclay.

"Except as you said she did seem to know your father terribly *well.*"

"An old family friend? when why not, well goodness!"

"So what d'you think then, in practice," the friend said, yawning in her little white swan throat.

"Dear love generation-wise I just *said*, she's Toby's father's second wife or whatever."

"Lissa *love*, what I meant was—"

"No but what I *meant* was, she said to me the thing was his immediate practical plans, where otherwise was he merely to stay poor old spoiled darling until he was even half-settled? so she'd sent her man who's this very good cook."

"But dearest turning over her whole butler or whoever to him like this?"

"Because she said it *upset* her to think of his trying to exist in hotels when their sheer service if nothing else would just start him yelling, as I must know."

"So then she knew him then obviously as I said!"

"Hm?"

"Will you *listen*?" her friend shrilled.

"What, dear?"

"Oh this years-ago affair they *must* have had, oh Lissa why can't you ever listen! when what other possible expl— "

"With *daddy*?" Melissa hooted. "Dear you *are* mad!"

"No but—"

"Why, there was *just nothing* in her manner!"

"Well sweet ninny of course not in *hers*!"

"Now dear tell me what else daddy's *ordinary* social manner is normally! I mean he goes on as if any woman he met were some lovely portrait to beam at or whatever."

"Oh their entire generation's simply too goa— too gallant for words, well admittedly," the friend babbled absently, squinting her lovely eyes to read her watch, at which she then muttered in anxiety, "—must *go*."

"Anyway she's not even near his age," Melissa announced.

"But everybody can't invariably have said no even in those days! in principle one's parents can have had these just dozens of affairs Lissa. Or do you think. Of course with their *contemporaries*."

"Twenty years ago?"

"So hard you mean to tell about customs then, well, mm."

"Why, she can't be even forty; dear I was amazed."

"So then he'll marry again anyhow you think."

"*My father?!*"

"Ptah Liss they all do."

" 'Always do,' why how can you know possibly, oh hideous!" she chattered, wild.

"Usually some sheerest bitch too," her worldliest friend told her.

"Why how can he!"

"Well Liss he *is* very good-looking. I mean in a distinguished way."

"Ah but then so darling, so just charming," that one mourned, bereft. "And when he does adore home so, poor wandering old love," she cried, as if wretched, "his precious box maze and his endless spreading green gloom of a beechwood and the old smokehouse we even *use*, dear can you imagine!"

"Though what will he do, I mean Liss in your view his plans. Because possibly you'd thought of taking a hand or d'you think."

"You can't mean *run* him!"

"Not 'run,' heaven! but this Mrs.—"

"Run *daddy*?" Melissa shrieked, in loving derision. "Or even hang over him like some groaning Greek chorus, chanting and admonishing, dearest you're unhinged!"

"Well, yes, *parents.*"

"Though with mummy deserting him admittedly I am involved; responsible even, if one has to use the word."

"Sam does, oh I could scream," his young wife whimpered, peering at her watch.

"Because I have to suggest things he can fill up his time with. Or just now anyway. For example I suggested why didn't he write his memoirs. Then I've been thinking of having him take Morgan out or whatever."

"*Your father?*"

"Sweetie she came to me frantic! you know how she is, so beset, if she goes out with the same boy three times in a row she *has* to break the sequence with a date with somebody else or it's terribly anti-magic for her, yet she isn't allowed to *refuse* the three-times one if he asks for a fourth date first. So she's defenseless."

"Yes why can't she have sensible magics like anybody? oh she's unstrung."

"Dearest she's *oral*-level, she says there has to be this genuine other date so she can *genuinely* refuse the three-times boy, so in consequence she's always frenziedly plotting after the second date with anyone because on the third they think the fourth's just automatic. So when she came to me half out of her mind with Toby absolutely *looming* and begged me to make daddy ask her out even for cocktails—well, after all, my own sister's roommate, dear! and when obviously it would also fill out an evening for him, or d'you think."

"Mm."

"He *loves* ordering meals and being exigent."

"Well dear I think you're heroic."

"Well admittedly he does have these rather serious debit sides, poor old at-loose-ends darling, he *yells* so and then every woman in sight leering hopingly at him since I was an infant in arms, just disgusting!"

"Oh, their manners, Liss."

"While uninterruptedly lecturing us on ours!"

"And *going on* so about sex and all right in front of one for years, so boasty!"

"So unfeeling!"

"Of course what else *is* there to think of really. But still, so irresponsible! and when one couldn't compete! Or wasn't supposed to, oh I despaired."

"Only what can mummy think she'll even find, compared I mean!" the indignant daughter burst out.

"Well Liss at that age."

"Why, daddy was so *amusing* merely! Simply his epigrams, for example now *wait*, I learned it by heart, his most-polished-ever he called it: 'I have spent my life making epigrams that apply to women and I have never yet found a woman they apply to' and he was *only twenty* when he thought it up!"

"Ah what must simply go on in their heads about us, practically," the friend let helplessly fall. "Why just *unsettling*!" she moaned.

"Why, twenty's what my mere baby brother is!"

"Nickie's twenty?"

"Dear *not* Nickie; my *baby* brother; I just *said*. Oh he's in this phase, he has these perfectly manic 'engagements,' dear I told you."

"Mm."

"He comes home all obsessed and ranting with these tales of how he's just proposed to some child in college and she's said yes! *sheerest* id-fantasy of course and naturally it turns out *she* not only wouldn't dream of marrying him but didn't even know he thought he was asking her to!"

" 'Engaged,' well just juvenile!"

"It's a *visitation*! mummy's driven beside herself by him!"

"Yes you said, mm."

"Though of course as to daddy, it isn't as if mummy'd ever known even to begin with how to handle *daddy*," Melissa said in contented disparagement.

But the friend grieved, "Ah though Lissa, as to handling them, how can one ever know, so unwarned, even what they'll think of to do."

"Impenetrable, mm."

"Ah *so* precarious, how know what they're ever like, when one's so lost in them; so helpless and all at bay."

"What, dear?"

"Oh Liss we *are* powerless, or d'you think."

"So then you mean how does one ever know one's 'handling' them at all, well dear *yes*."

"So therefore why won't they look after us more then, ah, the way we are," the lovely confidante mourned; adding sadly and softly to herself, "if they love us; *really* love ... " eyes now dreaming, unseeing, on what appeared to be her watch.

"So exhausting, so endless," Melissa started on.

But here her best adviser suddenly shrieked *look* at the time it was, she was lost, she must utterly *vanish*, springing up scattering tiresome lists like autumn leaves, Vallombrosa or anywhere for that matter, for as she bleated she was *utterly* late!! and scuttled.

Though when Melissa lightly called "Say buon giorno to him for me" into the hallway after her she yelped "Why who ever *said*!" stopped in her tracks, stricken, eyes suddenly huge; or stopped for one foundering moment anyway—before screaming back in airiest disparagement, "Oh, Liss, men, *coo* how oestrous!" this being beyond cavil universally established, even God's plan, que sais-je? and raced charmingly off.

Next day then Nicholas's dear daughter interrupted him in mid-feed by ringing him up if you please with some nonsensical hortatory supervising about his evenings.

Because she was *worried* about his just staying home in them merely because the food was better.

Because she was ringing him up even though she was on the point of rushing out to be lunched, which one's husband *didn't*, her father of course hadn't met this particular new man in their set but he'd roomed with Sam at Yale but then abroad for years but now back but terribly *interesting*, all involved at practically policy-level in that hushy échelon liaison with SHAPE and State and whoever they were at Fontainebleau when they were *there* (or at Bonn too for months at one period about which she was not free even to breathe) and in Fontainebleau her father would *approve* for he no less than drove a gig! well, being French, it was un wiski actually she supposed, with this smart little Tourangelle mare he'd won from the General on a bet he snickeringly refused to tell her what over, anyway her father would approve because here was a Yale man who *did* know how to order a meal properly, even magisterially, so she had in fact to fly out her door on mad wings that instant and *couldn't* be later already or more dithery, but she felt in his evenings he should overcome his feelings about this disgusting divorce and go *out*.

Why, he said, how sweet of her to be concerned! but he said was nightclub cuisine a form of stoicism he was prepared to dedicate even one evening to?

Not nightclubs but something like the St. Regis and what she'd thought was, with all his own contemporaries married and unavailable, obviously he should simply take out somebody young and hence not attached yet, it was only logical, Morgan for instance whom he knew fairly well already, also she danced beautifully which he loved—and he needn't sound stuffy and amazed like that, what could possibly be leveler-headed!

He said pretty doubtfully, why, he supposed he could have her in if she liked, but the trouble was—

But not *in*! because why couldn't he be his courtly old-sweetie self and just very angelically take her for once *out*? and *not* abuse the food. Because what did he think she meant was good for *him* if not out? what could he imagine? when for a woman this was an emphasis, it was like jewels; besides meaning in practice one could dress up, to be dazzling to him.

He said what about St. Regis food though, place be full of Texans wouldn't it? he'd heard the waiters yapped to one another audibly, and the maître d'hôtel— Where in New York could a man who knew about food eat anyway no matter what he paid out? ah well though, mustn't bore her with all that again, merely his customary strictures on the Creator's arrangements, shouldn't upset her—nor Him either, as far as he could see.

At which she quoted her great-grandmother at him: "I doubt whether thee upsets thy Creator as much as thee thinks thee does," this being a family jest; now she must *fly*, and hung up.

So when he got back to his lunch it was cold.

Thus he had to ring up Morgan disgruntled by this too, having (after a review of all tactical risks involved) settled with resignation on the Iridium Room after all: at least see it again, be nostalgically *in* the place—that much gloomy satisfaction anyhow amid this endless suicidal impermanence and demolishment, with nothing left to him as it had once been, or was.

So, wincing, he rang Morgan up. Said in his best courtly manner, would she take dinner with him? he meant tonight even; felt they might dance too if that worked in, she care to? and she said she would love to in tones of such simple happiness that when he'd hung up by god he found he'd not actually noticed before what a lovely young voice she had, what sapphire enchantments in it, what tender, what haunted promisings; as in fact he supposed however any bewitching little actress why not.

So anyhow.

So anyhow he called for her all charm mobilized, what's more in a fiacre from the plaza, which he decided would be full romantic fig for her years—actually, too, have been a simple pity not to, through the warm murmurous urban evening, the streetlamps hanging nodding like the blooms of great peonies in the gathering dusk, through this jewel-box twilight, and she by heaven a dazzle beside him half-naked in her summer black, with her eyes like stars for him, down Fifth Avenue to the Iridium Room— in the impossible anachronism of which he briskly got vermouths cassis ordered and, grabbing her little hand, shouldered their way into the packed and solid wall of dancing couples and took her in his arms.

In these she instantly leaned back to announce with shining eyes, "Oh Nicholas to *start* this evening of all evenings with a thing I never heard of, oh what angel luck!"

He answered with a kindly interrogative grunt, having spotted through the mob a distant pretty back.

Morgan said, "I bet you didn't even guess it was a First for me, what you ordered for us I mean."

"What, why, decent enough drink I suppose," he agreed, still absent. "New to you, huh; *well* now."

"And so sweet it's with you it's this First," she told him happily, clinging to him, as through the music's reiterated formal archways they began to turn and turn.

He explained, now paying attention, "Can't have you starting a hard evening's dalliance on champagne."

But she dreamed at him, saying "My omen," in radiant awe.

"Vermouth cassis? perfectly normal summer aperitif."

"Well I know it seems child— I mean it's not important to you and I know it Nicholas, just ordering a drink I've never had before or heard of, but you might try to see why for *me* it's a special happiness."

"Now what's this," he demanded uneasily.

She said in the lowest tone that would reach his ear, "Because for a woman every smallest thing from her lover has such new meanings," and put her face down on his shoulder. But when he instantly stiffened, just as swiftly she was lilting up at him in her gayest mode, "Well of course you're not technically my lover or any other way, are you, no matter how shamelessly I wish you

were, so you needn't defend yourself glaring like a bull, Nicholas!
Anyway Nicholas all I *meant*," she went meekly on, "was now i
will be one sweet secret thing more to remember whenever I order ;
vermouth cassis, which now will be always, I don't see why yo
should mind. Much less glower like that, ah *please* don't, if I'm
woman and can't help behaving the way we have to with you! A
you of all people know," she finished, with a soft look at him.

"Now what random informal feminine instruction's all this!"
exclaimed in general alarm.

"Well if you don't play Firsts you won't understand why, b
you must *see* that in threes they're omens! I mean if they work
you," she said soberly. "Well, so the very first thing you orde
for me the first time you ever took me dancing is my first taste o
so it's an omen."

"Well dammy now," he rumbled.

"Which means I can stop *working* at you in such agonies
what I hope it's an omen about. Because now all I want will
happen of itself, oh Nicholas imagine! Without my having to d
myself frantic dragooning you!"

"Why, fine!" he said, not understanding any of this.

She said in a voice as soft as a breath "oh my dearest" and
tled her cheek in sighing repossession of his collarbone.

So the band went into some Bantu business or other with th
of Greasy-Toe Stomp. "Though I bet even now you haven't
ted the *main* three Firsts, Nicholas," she went on then.

"Not, huh."

"It even interlocks with the set I just told you about. '
makes it stronger and more binding still, oh my darling you'
rounded!" she sang in tender exultation, eyes aglow.

"Now what unbelted b.j. species of—"

"Well obviously, first, it's our first rendezvous isn't it! I
that isn't the word but it's the *thing* Nicholas; and next, t'
thing you did on this First was dance with me, for the firs
That makes two. And *this* second First I'm in your arms
interrupt, *I am*! and even this formally it still counts, I bet
anyhow believe in symbols, Nicholas, just as frantically as I

So beginning to laugh he asked then what was her third.

"Well it's something you haven't noticed. Or I don't th
have."

"Pretty extrasensory type though," he said amiably, patting her.

"But if I tell you, I don't know what you'll do, can't you see?" she cried tensely. "Only if I *don't* maybe then it spoils the omen!"

"So you see you do have to tell me then," he summed up, as the band slid along toppling melancholy walls of sound into Yo Sho Pick A Hot Tahm To Cool Off.

"But it's about how you are *toward* me, Nicholas, and if I tell you you'll change, oh how can I, I can't!" she wept in a swoon of misery deep there in his arms, as through the unassembled shards of the music, its bare ruined choirs, they suitably turned and turned.

"Now *now*," he consoled her, for whatever it was. (Beyond *him*!)

She gazed at him with great misty eyes, gulping.

So he prompted, "So now then what."

"Well if I have to tell you," she said in a choking voice, "it's that this is the first time, in all these months I've loved you so blindingly, that you've ever once *really* treated me as if I were even nice enough to more than politely glance at," and buried her face in his shoulder, clinging.

"But my dear little thing but good *god*!" he cried, stunned, "why what possibly, now you can't mean I've been some damn' brute!"

She flashed one range-finding look at him and hid again, moaning something too stricken to be articulate.

"Now my sweet child!" he implored her.

To this she replied, still muffled, by pronouncing his name as if it were music.

"Now dammit Morgan—"

She wailed, "Oh you've wounded me so! Because you really *hadn't* noticed, had you," she accused him, flinging up her head and staring at him with great wet eyes, "but tonight you've been so sweet and wonderful, only now you've made me tell you you'll change, it's all spoiled, you'll be *conscious* of it, you'll probably even start hating me for not leaving it unsaid," she ended in piteous tones.

"I swear I—"

"Oh Nicholas I so didn't want to upset you tonight, on this first night of all nights, I didn't even intend to harass you by telling you I love you."

" 'Harass'!" he echoed, taken aback still again.

"Well, I had it planned to be just docile and *happy* with you, if you must know. Anyhow not like the—that morning," she amended, dropping her eyes. "Oh Nicholas I know I've fought you and dragooned you and driven you, and I've thrown myself at you, but now I'm not going to again, ever. I am just going to be yours. And *obey* you Nicholas. Anyhow now I have my lovely omen," she cooed contentedly.

" 'Surrounded,' huh!" he said in amusement.

"Well it can't upset you, because you don't believe in it! So you can't object to my using it, so there!"

"Necromancy by god!"

"Then I can *have* my omen? even if it snares you for me?" she laughed in a voice all jewels.

"Why, snared already I expect, why not, only gentlemanly course open," he conceded, "though now how about drinking the thing for once," and took her back to their table.

So they sat; and next, lifting her glass to his she said shyly, "Well it *is* the first time and you don't really mind after all," then sipping she cried out, "Why, it's delicious!" in surprise.

He mildly teased her, " 'Mind,' why should I 'mind,' pretty guilty little conscience to think so!"

"Well then it slipped out," she muttered, faintly pink; but at once adding, "Well you know as well as I do, Nicholas, it's just that I *am* so yours that I can't hide anything I ought to. I have no pride with you. Which is why I have so much trouble controlling you, damn it!" she burst out.

Nicholas snagged a waiter who was catapulting past and told him bring two more vermouths cassis, and the confounded menu while he was at it.

"Because men doing what I want them's no problem, heavens. But you, Nicholas, are just infuriating," she said in tones of adoration. "But if I do tell you all my humiliating secrets, and I *do*, Nicholas," she pleaded, practically as if this were so, "Can't you see it's because I am trying to display *every* side of what I am like for your approval, hoping there'll be something somewhere to please you?''

"You ought to, huh, study my old namesake's portraits of ladies,'' he threw in distractedly, as couples inched bumping past them from the dance-floor, for the music had now stopped.

She buried her little nose in her drink and stared at him over the rim in bafflement and dudgeon.

"Not from Wiltshire, that Romney,'' this Romney said, "but I mean to say he picked some damn' delicious women to sit to him. As every brush-stroke makes plain he knew, too!''

In a flash she'd set down her glass and cried in rapture, "Oh my dearest then it *wasn't* spoiled!''

He gaped.

"I mean you do like me, you really do!''

"*Well* now!'' he growled.

"Well you think I'm pretty!''

And before he could open his mouth in reply, "Oh think, I'm *good* for you!'' she crooned in happy wonder, stretching her young arms to him over the gleaming white and silver of their table.

He groaned, "Well you're a mad sex,'' taking in his fingers one elegant little wrist, which he pawed tenderly.

"But Nicholas you don't know about *me* yet, really,'' she eagerly went on.

"Different, huh.''

She snatched her wrist away crying, "You don't have to gloat at me, I *know* you think all women are alike, Melissa warned me, oh I think it's horrifying!''

" 'Melissa'!''

"Well, she told the way you make these cold-hearted epigrams about us, oh I know they're witty but when I love you like this they make my heart *sink*, my darling!''

He blandly quoted himself: "Women, like tragedy, should inspire pity and terror.''

"*You see?*'' she bleated.

"Made 'em in French too at one time, she tell you? La faiblesse des femmes n'est pas qu'elles se laissent persuader mais qu'elles se persuadent elles-mêmes for example; quite true too.''

Into her eyes there sprang great clear tears.

"*Now* what've I said, oh what an impossible damn' sex,'' he bayed. "Look dammit I made the thing up *in college*, you weren't even born when I m— "

"It isn't the *things* you say that wound me," she said very low, blinking bravely, "oh my dearest what hurts so is that how I feel isn't even enough on your mind to make you see how they'll wound me when you say them."

"Now you know quite well," he was beginning at her when the band threw up a sudden wild fountain of sound, any practical lighting went out, and in the embellished gloom a big luscious bangled girl sprang onto the dance-floor under a dizzying spotlight and began singing Got No Budder Onto It, in niggra.

When this din was over Nicholas clobbered a waiter and got the goddam menu. But the young woman at once came demurely back onto the floor and to what sounded like Haydn with grave charm sang

> What laurels, ah, what sauntering thighs are these,
> What sweets profundive to dismay

or whatever the actual words were. Everybody with any culture applauded this in riot; so for an encore this babe flaunted her handsome way through

> Caint git started wid de fuss-class tidings,
> Caint git goin' wid de glow-ry news

waving a bustle that gently broke a man's heart.

"She's *pretty*!" Morgan raged in a whisper. "I bet you think so, too!" she cried, eyes on the woman like knives.

"Hardly be simple-minded enough to say so, huh."

"So you do so then!" she gasped, stricken. "You think she's *desirable*!"

"What's this? now dammy I hardly as much as—"

She drooped, lamenting. "No but Nicholas I do have to find out what you really like, can't you see?"

"Some *singer*?" he demanded incredulously.

"Oh Nicholas please you aren't just lying to me again?"

" 'Lying'!"

"Well I never have any security with you, you know it! Oh but tonight I wasn't going to reproach you! Oh Nicholas I'm truly *not* reproaching you! Even for playing safe by bringing me here.

Instead of some small elegant restaurant where I could be alone
with you. The way I'd pl— dreamed it.''

"Why see here," he instantly said (having prepared this much
anyhow), "I brought you here especially, to dance with you."

"Oh Nicholas, did you really, oh darling! Oh but how can I be
sure you did! Because *did* you?''

"Dance for instance right now," he suggested smoothly, as the
band's brass blew a preluding fanfare.

"Even if you didn't, you said it to make me happy," she whispered.

"So then come on," he boomed, standing up. The band plunged
into some moody nostalgia out of the early Thirties:

> O honey
> Honeyhoney
> Lil ca'iage-trade honey
> What de good word
> Fum
> Heah
> On
> Down

They danced. She murmured from the blest bower of his arms,
"So you do like me. Enough to be willing to be kind to me. To *recognize* that I do love you. So see? I'm saying the so-see to myself," she purred up at him, and stretching radiantly up kissed a
corner of his jaw with her soft little mouth. And then back again
against his collarbone.

Though immediately turning up this perfectly teasing face to
misexplain to him, "Just trying to palliate the harshness of your
circumstances, my darling!''

—So in a word he didn't get home and into bed till God knows
what hour.

He was hardly up, midmorning next day, when round his Victoria
came as if she'd never addressed an unadoring syllable to him
"—to see for one split second how you simply are, Nicholas!'' she

announced in brightest tones and not looking at him at all, eluding his embrace by neatly popping into it an armful of small parcels.

And on lightly past him into the back drawing-room. Here she struck an amorous chord on the piano and cried, "Make sure for *myself* you're being well taken care of, poor unhinged darling!" before fluttering back and across to the chimney-piece in the front drawing-room, where she straightened the Copley ancestor, who was already straight.

Nicholas dumped the damn' parcels into a chair and took her by the shoulders and pulled her around (while she indulgently reminded him her car *couldn't* wait, blocking everything) and for a moment got his enchanting maddening creature in his arms; but these, after one brilliant look at him, she placatingly squirmed out of and ran out into the little garden, crying out tenderly he must have the piano *tuned*, and, next, that the flowers, as he must have seen for himself, what there was of them, were past their glorious prime. To which he naturally replied that she had made him so wretched he hadn't slept a wink for these *two nights* after the way she'd left the party, if she wanted the truth!

At this she conceded in happy tones, "Now I've merely run by to see how you're getting on," and tripped into the house again, where this time when he caught her he held her. So for some minutes they stood there while she gently murmured from against his heart the roll-call of her immediate engagements, and he described his agonies.

Until eventually she did have to go, *really* must, she assured him, so many things merely to do before even lunch; and drew lingeringly away and out of his arms, to the piano-bench, whither he at once followed. So there she butted her forehead against his shoulder while they disputed dreamily on.

For how could he consider constantly embroiling her, could he think of nothing but selfishly complicating her life? and when at this he groaned well where then by heaven had she gone after the party, leaving him desolate! she thrust herself away exclaiming did he for one peremptory moment mean she was to have developed no life of her own in these seventeen years he'd deserted her in? had she no duty no responsibility to herself? to her sweet fifth-former son? or did he dare hope she would now be light-minded because *then* she had been!

And when he begged her to explain why she kept repeating this 'deserted' when she knew the real reason as well as he? she instantly cried, shushing him, if he was going to be odious to her, did he want her never to be able to come visit him again!

Though now she was here, she said perhaps he would try to explain to her what he had been up to in the kitchen with that unstable little thing of her stepson's, poor boy.

He said if she cared for a candid answer the question struck him as being not what he but what the girl'd been up to.

But what had this still undefined activity been? which was what she'd asked.

Hiding she meant in the kitchen? to rouse that hulk of a boy to chasing her, he supposed she meant. Or did she mean the girl was a shade tight? Or even, as she'd suggested, unstable. Or upset or—

Mrs. Barclay said in a glossy tone the girl upset? on the contrary it had seemed to her that he, rather, had been rattled-sounding. So unlike him, she went on in affectionate concern. Because how could he at his age be upset by this ingénue, this child!

He said, beginning to laugh, he'd always hoped in his modest way he was attractive, now'd she claim he was even a menace to schoolgirls?

She said whether "schoolgirl" as he put it was a relevant category was a datum she did not possess; but what was not clear (she continued, meekly buttoning her top blouse-button which he had just undone), not clear to her anyway, nothing in the whole odd little episode was clear—Now merely where had he met this child before? since perhaps he had better fall back on some simpler presentation, for example chronological order which after all she said had its advocates.

So he affectionately unbuttoned the button again and said wasn't it plain? the girl was some school friend of his younger daughter's apparently. Been in this weekend party at West Chester, it seemed. Flunked out of Radcliffe freshman year, he now recalled being told. What possible aesthetic or sociological end was served by her buttoning it again? Though why they'd taken this particular girl in the first place heaven knew: madwomen!

This she said disengaging herself slightly might be part of a dean's history of Radcliffe, assuming such a book was printable, but did he think it fully explained what he pretended to be explaining? Buttoning it moreover was not a sociological question but a matter of his immaturity and childishness, which were incurable.

He cried out that to shut so heavenly a bosom from the sight of a man who adored both it and her was the act of a pig; furthermore if she held that the desire of male for female was proper only to the years before puberty how did she propose to explain the reproduction of the species? So she permitted him to kiss her lightly, smiling; and got him narrating again.

Except what was there to tell? The narrative was no narrative at all, simply this house-party afternoon, a cold dull-crimson after-glare from a November sunset and this house-party of kids had come straggling up from the stables through the autumn dusk in their mired riding-clothes and clumped stiffly into the library for tea (*late*, he need hardly inform her!), Morgan he recalled hand-in-hand with some gangling boy or other; she'd had on a dead-black turtleneck sweater and her boots and breeches and face mud-splashed, and as far as he could remember not even lipstick.

Mrs. Barclay said in an unexpected tone she was pleased to see that after eighteen years he had at last, if abruptly, learned to observe what a woman was wearing.

Huh? a visual memory he'd had all his life? why, he could — But anyhow! This girl— Well, when introduced she'd given him one of those long sultry looks that experience had taught him wasn't sultry but just near-sighted, and then turned her little back on him and loitered over to where her young man was slouched on the padded fender and sat down close beside him with her hand in his pocket. Well, it was an indecent unreticent generation by heaven! and he thanked God his own children didn't behave like some of their friends! Would she have the simple womanly decency to keep her pretty hands *off* a button he'd just arranged to his satisfaction? Anyhow this girl'd sat there with her temple lolled against the boy's bony young shoulder and as far as he could recall not a word out of her. So that was it. Hardly seen her again. Boy he presumed had monopolized her all the weekend. Or she him, depending on which sex it was sank its delighted fangs in the other.

Mrs. Barclay wished he had somehow learned to distinguish between a woman and an entree.

He said an entree has no buttons. So he'd never seen the girl again.

What did he mean by his 'never'?

Oh, well, yes, come to think of it, yes, he'd taken her with some of the others on a little tour of the valley farm and let her drive tractor for the tree-planter for a few furrows when she'd asked to. So then that was the whole story. Now why didn't she like the angel she was stay have lunch with him.

'*Lunch*'!

Yes, he'd ordered a particularly pleasant—

Lunch *today*?! when he'd already utterly thrown out her schedule with his evasions? her car waiting hours! And she herself waiting too, for him to finish this curious little story of his!

He said 'finish,' how'd she mean.

Its point. How it had gone on.

But pointless was just what the story was, he'd told her that to begin with!

Because all one had to do was glance at his great dissembling face, she answered him smiling, to see that there had been something more.

Point? there'd been no— Unless you could say, he supposed, that there had been one *time* more that he'd seen the girl that weekend, if that was the point, strictly speaking, that is, come to think of it, if that was what she meant; the girl having, uh, kissed him goodbye Monday morning she mean that? for what kind of a nugatory point was that!

Mrs. Barclay said 'nugatory' was hardly the adjective she would have expected him to choose when it was obvious there were others.

What? why it was a routine thing! He'd just settled himself at the wheel, there in the porte-cochère, to drive to the Bank as usual, why, this was something he did every morning! And she'd merely appeared beside the car. And bent down and in, without a word. And, well, huh, for the space of two bewildering heartbeats laid her mouth on his. There in the sleek hanging tent of her hair. And was gone!

And *before* she framed a comment let him point out to her, how routine! A mere bread-and-butter kiss! Or, all right, 'impetuous' then! He'd concede that; concede even that the girl had behaved a bit like a, well, like a Celt perhaps, for he supposed any jeune fille bien élevée would hardly have had the—

Mrs. Barclay at this gave a pretty little musical cry.

Now what? what did that mean! he besought her, taken aback.

Oh had he to be told?

She'd *laughed*?

Well, she was amused. He amused her.

'Amused' her!

She was amused by his fussy distinctions.

'Fussy'!

Could he do nothing but repeat her words back at her in this gaping way? His scruples, then! It would amuse any woman!

His scruples! when to the contrary it was the *girl's* want of modesty that—

Mrs. Barclay cooed at him he didn't really have the least notion, had he, how a woman's mind worked.

—So it was sheer luck that he could counter, leaning tenderly toward her, was she really bothered then, heavenly thing that she was? and was she at long last ready to ravish his senses by admitting it? Though if she meant had he at his age bewitched the child, well, why shouldn't he have? he asked her agreeably, weren't the textbooks full of such cases? Or did she like everyone else, at the first genuine sign of our most normal of passions, propose to summon in psychiatry and sociology! And turn *those* appalling fellows loose on our rituals of reproduction as well? with Nicholas Romney lectured by some whinnying percentage-monger on the statistical norms of love!

And she knew they'd just maintain (and here he finally began to smile) that every girl who'd ever loved him had done so because she was maladjusted, in fact that he was merely one of the charming thing's symptoms! And if this was alleged universally (as it was) had she reflected that its significance was therefore zero? and laughing contentedly into her now faintly smiling face he begged her to instruct him what medical excuse she herself felt able to proffer, what specific psychopathology, for the loveliest moments a woman's sweetness had ever conferred upon a man, those days and nights she had loved him, as never anyone before or he hoped since; nor would she, she must know as well as he, until she consented to love him once again.

And so on and so on until like an angel she stayed for lunch.

Moreover next day she dropped in for the briefest moment more, between a hair-dresser and a fitting, to have tea with him.

Or rather, since he hadn't intended going to the trouble of making tea, it being the man's afternoon out (Oh was it? so it was! she cried in pretty surprise), did she see any real grounds for not starting in on the evening champagne a shade earlier than usual? so presently she followed him tractably down to the kitchen to ice it.

Because she said she really could not (surely he saw for himself!) go on with this silliness of kissing him minutes at a time on every occasion she merely ran by to see him for fifteen seconds: she was fond of him, she was even indulgent, but couldn't he be serious? for she was so fond of him she hated to see him without plans.

No plans? he laughed, grabbing her again, when just the sight of her—

She pulled away crying he put her out of all patience! frivolous and intemperate as he was, when she was kind to him to his heart's content! had he come down to ice champagne or hadn't he?

So he had to clatter down to the wine-cellar and fetch a bottle and set to chopping ice.

Because she said smiling again didn't he think so too? which was another reason she'd had for coming back again to see him again so soon; or did he intend to spend his life philandering in kitchens, so irresponsible.

He said would she in her heaven-sent way fetch him the wine-cooler from the dining-room? from the sideboard. He supposed she was talking about that girl again, what was her name. *In* the sideboard, then. Whom he'd hardly more than met!

Neither on the sideboard nor in it but in the chimney-cupboard, she informed him, and brought it forgivingly; what she meant was he must not think he could have everything both ways.

He snorted now now, what was the use of being born into the privileged classes if one couldn't have it both ways? Had Mrs. Barclay herself at a party never agreeably trifled with her host's sensibility if only from good manners? and forgot the whole thing in a quarter-hour! Probably a high percentage of our national passes were made in kitchens anyhow, had to be made somewhere! Though this girl hadn't done anything of the kind!

'Done,' Mrs. Barclay mimicked him, what had 'done' to do with it, she quoted unfeelingly; as if what an experienced little actress decided she wanted to implant in his head were to be given the status of evidence!

He said dammit no man with fifty years' astonished acquaintance with female conduct was going to wear down his imagination guessing why a young woman leaned wordlessly against him in a kitchen to inform him she found him temporarily fetching! Girls had no judgment; they had a political talent, but common sense, no; moreover they looked only at that part of the future, even at that part of the next five minutes, that suited their dreamy fancy. It was cool enough to sip now, should they take it up to the drawing-room?

So they went up, she inquiring in a special tone what did he mean by 'wordlessly'? and he arguing that girls of twenty of course spoke but what did they ever say in so many words.

For he said had Mrs. Barclay herself at that age in similar circumstances for example— Suppose she'd temporarily set her panting heart on a wary man of fifty, why, if she opened her little red mouth she'd just find herself out-argued. Now here: the wine was beautifully cool. Whereas the ambiguities of a throbbing silence, how unanswerable! Nor was it something she need snort about, did she really think?

She had *anything* but snorted!

And did she have to fuss at him like this over something that hadn't even *happened* good god? just when the champagne was cool? when how was *he* responsible for some pretty child's moods!

Mrs. Barclay asked in a hardly temperate tone whether he actually wished her to believe him such a dolt as to think himself helpless—at his age! and with what she blushed at having to refer to as his experience!—helpless against any random misconduct of any common little thing that flung herself at his irresponsible head?

'Flung'? when she must know the whole roster of alternate motivations as well as he did:—The girl'd been temporarily separated from what's-his-name, Toby, and wanted to touch something male. Or it was just the end of a long day and she felt down. Or she felt dramatic. Or it had been a mere *game* then, dammit! enfin tout le bazar! Or with a young actress doubtless the phrase was toute la comédie. Or a mere bet with herself! Or even simply she wanted to make him admit she was femalely *there*, why not! And Mrs. Barclay needn't make that pretty pouting face, had she forgotten the time she herself, in this very kitchen—

Would she drink her drink and stop this flouncing? for even on the preposterous hypothesis that the girl had for fifteen seconds conceived a passion for him, did that alter the fundamental fact that it was *she*, Mrs. Barclay, that he single-heartedly adored? *Well*, then!

For ah, these memoirs she'd suggested he write, what would they be (assuming he wrote them) but a record of her? And need she look at him with such sadness? was it "sad" that there was no woman on earth he had loved like this? For to revise the metaphor what was his memory but a gallery of portraits of her!

And refilled their glasses, sighing.

So in order to sip this round comfortably they sat on the piano-bench.

His whole mind a gallery, Victoria after Victoria framed side by side, this radiant girl (he droned in tenderest persuasiveness), eyes looking their happy questions out at him from whatever irrelevant chiaroscuro of a background it was, the wedding they'd first met at, the Brevoort terrasse; the same breath-taking girl on and on à perte de vue in new frames and new poses and other costumes and often no costume on by god at all thank God! he ended in a meatier tone, seizing her free hand.

Which barely fussing she seemed to decide to let him have.

For how constantly his memory saw her as if coming to meet

him, emerging for *him* out of whatever landscape his mind painted, along this or that elegant Palladian perspective—

At which tender and time-confounding point the goddam phone rang and it was his tomcat of a son!

"You're *what*!" this father bellowed.

".....”

"But what the devil are you doing in Northampton of all pos— "

".....”

"Met *which* young woman of yours, doesn't it by god occur to you I may have quite enough trouble keeping track of my own?"

".....”

"Still more recent even than *that* one, I see!"

".....”

"Um."

".....”

"She *what*?"

".....”

" 'Platonism'!"

".....”

"But good heavens Nickie—"

".....”

"Well but is the child in love with this goddam associate professor of philosophy or with *you*?"

".....”

"No, but what earthly—"

".....”

"Nothing special about your particular generation, it'd make no sense in *any* era!"

".....”

"Then what *is* the nature of this unfathomable understanding or whatever the hell it is you succeed in not explaining!"

".....”

"But look here Nickie, any girl that falls in love with men old enough to be her father—"

".....”

"Now Nickie my dear boy if I may for one moment interpose a—"

".....”

"No but I wonder whether you'll mind my making a sug— my asking a question of a most benevolent kind. A most *concerned* kind, Nickie, if I may put it in an old-fashioned way; I mean this is none of my business at all. But my point is: now, you're going to Italy this summer. Now, as you know—"

". . . . ."

'Well *exactly* Nickie, only I meant a *nice* Italian girl."

". . . . ."

"What the devil does that tone mean!"

". . . . ."

"Well for one thing they're female by god!"

". . . . ."

"*I* know American girls are female!"

". . . . ."

"Well, European girls don't go around behaving as if the fact unnerved them so!"

". . . . ."

"This one doesn't, uh."

". . . . ."

"Oh, she is? I see."

". . . . ."

"Is, huh; *well*!"

". . . . ."

"I know, I know, but a really nice Ital— "

". . . . ."

"For one thing they were civilized when our own Sassenach ancestors were still rutting around in caves!"

". . . . ."

"Ah well, as civilized as girls are ever likely to be; my point is—"

". . . . ."

"*Need* variety, goddammit!"

". . . . ."

"The hell with progressive education!"

And so on, declaring to this idiot boy that if God, or Iddio rather, ever put an inclination for him into some lovely little Roman head he'd assure him he'd never say a disrespectful thing about Him again, perfect old *angel* by god was what he'd call Him! and so on and so on. So by the time the damn' boy had rung off, Victoria had of course literally to fly to her fitting.

✥

Accordingly he was boring the hell out of himself that evening over some piece of current arrière-avantgarde fiction or other (who'd guess there had ever been a time when the subject of fiction was simply Achilles? before all these interior decorators turned author! or before we had all these standard Southern masterpieces, all disembowelings and relatives with two heads), when the door-pull sounded in his empty house and there on his doorstep in the deep June night was his obed^t little serv^t Morgan.

Who at once with a tender air of appeasement stepped in and stood in his arms lifting her mouth with meek assurance to be kissed.

" ... so see darling?" she murmured in time then, taking that sweet young mouth gently away from him at last; and when he rumbled some sort of reply, unlocked his embrace by submissive degrees, lingering still; but ultimately on into the drawing-room, he following, while she sighed to him, "I suppose you'll want some *explanation* Nicholas, when all I'm really doing is stop by for five minutes, well who'd explain that?" and in the pier-glass between the front windows smiled placatingly into his reflected eyes.

"Though couldn't the whole reason," she softly cried, turning to him, "just be the sheer luxury of not being held off at a distance at last any longer?—being able to come to you in this heavenly peace? Or was that actually what you meant, my dearest?"

Whatever he replied to this was still too far on the gruff side to be made out.

"I mean what you said when you took me dancing, about a serious talk," she explained things to him.

At this, starting to laugh, he told her if she recalled her Dante, quel giorno più there'd been precious little serious talk!

"Well I don't know what you're talking about but it was just too sweet an evening to be serious," she said in happy accents, sinking into his chair. "So now I came by in case you still wanted to be," she expounded further, picking up and sampling a sip from his half-empty glass, which she made a face at and set down.

So he offered, get her a drink?

"No because I'm not going to *stay*, Nicholas. Though as you might guess this 'serious talk' was a reason I stopped by."

He said *what* serious talk!

"Or partly was. Or Nicholas if you still really want one. Oh if you knew how sweet it is to be able to tell you anything and everything! Because I also came, partly, if you insist on knowing, because my psychiatrist advised against it."

He mildly resounded.

"Well *of course* I'm seeing a psychiatrist about you! For months and months! After what you did to me that morning—why, you Rejected me!" she reproached him, in indignant technicality. "Well actually she's a woman psychiatrist and you can sneer but she understands me Nicholas! Oh will *you* some day? Though she did do just what you predicted she would!" she cooed in sudden derision.

He asked her, rather staggered, how could he have foreseen the behavior of this woman when he'd not even foreseen the prerequisite likelihood of her existence?

"Well I remember *everything* you've said!" she cried at him in loving surprise, "and you said *this* that weekend at West Chester the day we had lunch champêtre deep in that wonderful grove of beeches stretching on and on and on, by that half-ruined Doric folly with its frusts and columns."

He said actually, he believed, it was Corinthian if anything. Also perhaps she meant the pieducci.

"Well *anyway* Nicholas you were yelling at Melissa and her husband, and at Nickie too partly, about psychiatrists, and you said that if for instance a girl was no-matter-how bored with her husband and in love with somebody else, still the average psychiatrist didn't 'pay the most rudimentary attention to these *facts*' (was how you said it), he just shooed her back to her husband, because no matter what they *say*, you said what they *do* is prescribe as if the ideal course is for everybody to be exactly and endlessly like everybody else and only do what everybody else thinks should be done, 'adjusted,' and you were outraged."

He said who wouldn't be? unless she cared to except Immanuel Kant!

"So sure enough *she* tried to shoo me back toward Toby and I just *hooted*!"

Nicholas civilly snorted too, and lugged his glass back to the cellaret.

"So she went *very* stiff, could I have just one vermouth cassis then?" she begged, coming to stand obediently beside him. "So I can have my third on my first peaceful loving visit to you," she explained, resting her cheek shyly against his big arm. "Still she does sympathize, Nicholas."

He said *fine*; and in addition, that he was delighted to hear it.

"Though Nicholas she did make this hilariously un-psychiatrist remark! It was once when I was weeping my heart out over you in her office, and she said, 'My dear, I too have loved and lost,' *imagine*!"

He said the woman should transfer her God-given inabilities to some less taxing sphere.

"Well of course she lost! I mean she dresses beautifully but Nicholas she looks just like a sweet little pouter pigeon!" she exulted, and in one swift whirl curvetting away from him to the pierglass gazed with love at the smiling beauty poised in the shadowy depths there. "Oh but will you *truthfully* answer me something?" she cried.

Why, he'd never lied to a pretty girl in his life!

"Well, 'pretty,' Nicholas you've already granted that much you know, and anyway I *am*; but what I want you to admit," she instructed him, eyes still wide with delight at that glowing young image, "is, don't you secretly *like* having somebody this pretty in love with you like this?"

So in common decency what else could he by god say?

She whispered trembling, "Ah you do you *do*, oh Nicholas dance with me!" stepping in luxury into his arms, and (the lack of any music being evident enough to both of them) stood there as in happy swoon.

But he quickly said, patting her—and might he for one moment switch back a little in all this? to something she'd said just before?—he said of course the woman appeared to have a chiefly statistical and textbook knowledge of the human heart, and certainly very little talent for expressing what information she did possess: no one would agree more than he on her lack of competence. But on the other hand Morgan must not over-simplify either! and in short what about this undiscussed question of what-was-his-name? her young man.

This, she glided effortlessly past at once: "Oh but *now* Nicholas? when it might take hours, when after all I'm just here for these two minutes luxuriating in your not being all solemn and formidable with me Nicholas darling. And when anyhow the real reason I dropped by is something I thought of that I bet you never in the world would guess but I hope will please you."

He nevertheless, he said, saw no reason—

But she ran on in tones of adoration, "Oh Nicholas I've been so wanting to think of something I could do for you that no other woman's ever done, something you'd *accept* my doing I mean, and this afternoon I thought of it!"

And while his mind tried to deal with this, prattled on, "Well, I know it may not seem like much to you, but little things are *important* things to a woman, Nicholas, if only you knew enough about us to understand; and this is just that nose-jewel."

He said blankly now when on earth had he told her about *that* early piece of amatory fol-de-rol!

"Why Nicholas how can you possibly need reminding?" she cried in disbelief, "why, it was coming back from the tree-planting thing, you *can't* forget walking me back all that way with my arm through yours! when naturally I'd let the others get ahead. So you were grumbling about food in Princeton at first, at your Reunions, but then you began about the girls the seniors had flocking round at commencement or whenever it was, fiancees and sisters too you supposed, and your first impression had been my *god* what hundreds of pretty young girls but then you'd seen that it was just that they were young. So my heart sank; except I knew I *was* pretty; and also I knew I could somehow make you notice it eventually, as a matter of fact I thought you possibly had already but were too stiff to admit it to yourself, I mean here you were walking with me weren't you? so by this time you were saying you'd got used to looking at your sons' classmates and seeing they looked exactly like your own classmates decades ago, but it was a *shock* when you found yourself doing the same thing with girls, looking at this shining little head or that melting slope of shoulder (you said) and realizing that what you were seeing was not this girl here in 1958 but someone who'd looked just like her only it'd been 1931! of course with a different hair-do, you admitted. 'I mean to say boys, who gives a damn about boys,' you said, 'but when I start seeing *girls* in this how-like-your-breath-taking-mother-you-are sort of way ... !' —so you see I decided they did please you, then, so I was in heaven, for I thought oh then *I*'d please you even more, I mean being prettier, and oh I clung so softly and with such hope to your arm—the first time ever, oh Nicholas I'd never been so close to you before! Only then you began grumbling about their tenue, these girls', Bermuda shorts and so on, you said where had all the baroque charm gone? and you said for example you wanted a sweet dessert to be really and elaborately *sweet*, no nonsense about de-cloying it, and in the same way a pretty girl ought to—but then you broke off and began to laugh and said here you'd spent a lifetime trying to persuade one pretty woman after another to even just occasionally wear those nose-jewels that made Hindu women look so delicious, you'd actually had one made up years ago, a tiny clustering rose of diamonds that clipped gently on with a little spring-clip like an earring's, but not one woman would wear it for you, not even to give you two minutes' delight looking at her beauty with it on. Only then there we were at the house and everybody out front waiting for us so I had to let go your arm before we'd crossed even that threshold together, oh how *easy* it is to tell you all this or anything, my dearest, now that you're almost ready to love me a little at last!'' she said happily, smiling into his eyes.

He at once replied that while he couldn't say he recalled all this in, uh, quite such unerring detail, still, if a lifetime's delight in the mere look, the mere tournure, of women, in the posed and lovely portraits they always somehow made him half-think they were—

"Oh Nicholas *please*, I'm not 'women,' I'm—''

He told her now wait, he'd been about to recite and translate for her a verse of Ovid's, that went

> saepe tepent alii iuvenes, ego semper amavi

which he'd render 'Can't answer for my tepid competitors, but I've always been in love with some agreeable woman or other,' he assured her; and perhaps, he said he meant, it was just this that she must not be tempted to misinterpret.

To this piece of delicacy she paid no attention(except for five seconds to gaze into her drink instead of at him), meekly saying, "So then you must still have it then, your lovely jewel I mean."

Well he supposed naturally he did somewhere or other.

"I mean here *with* you Nicholas, in this house?"

He asked her sighing now how could he be sure about the answer to a question of that sort without prolonged and thorough-going search? what with these masses of baggage and boxes and what-all this miserable domestic crisis of his had forced upon him.

"You couldn't have just this one *quick* look in a place you'd *probably* have put it, Nicholas, like a jewel-box?"

So he said with a snort of laughter she certainly did want to try the bauble on didn't she! and when he fetched his stud-box there of course it was in plain sight right on top among cuff-links and studs, this small white blazing rose.

Which he picked out and dropped in her palm, and she took with a little soft sound of wonder and delight and flew to the pier-glass. And slipped it on, submissively muttering "ow."

Now she saw what he meant? he cried in self-approbation, justified: see how delicious she looked in the thing, what it did for a charming nostril!

Tilting her enchanted head in this pose and that, she pored in a passion over this new image the glass held poised there, saying "oh Nicholas oh think" meanwhile in no particular tone.

Well was she convinced?

"Well it's the most uncomfortable thing I ever wore in my life if you must know darling," she told him lovingly. "But you see I wear it for you, no *other* woman ever did! Only I do everything I do merely to please you, can't you tell that by now?"

And running to him begged, "Oh shall I wear it for you, my dearest? Oh Nicholas shall I?"

So he said, laughing, settle for that would she, huh! battle if not the war?

But laughing, glittering, back, "Why you're not even *pretending* to fuss!" she cried in angel complicity; and shortly thereupon wore the bauble home.

✌❧

Melissa said at lunch at Il Baloccone, scooping from her melon rose-pink cusps, to her dearest friend (who was eating a sfogliata) that all things considered she had now decided, poor old sweet, to pack her father off almost at once to Europe, or in practice she supposed Paris, this being the classic "return" for his generation, they'd never set foot in Italy.

"Because I had this perfectly penetrating feeling he wants to be *alone*," she theorized. "I mean who at his age doesn't, do they, so he must. No responsibilities and just *enjoy* himself, so when he rang me up and said he'd decided to go abroad, even fairly soon, well I said I *agreed*. So possibly he's going."

"To be out of the way for her divorce you mean too, oh I see," the friend said, in antistrophe.

"Yes, when now he has just nobody."

"Also when your mother marries whoever."

"Dearest *your* hypothesis not mine! because as I told you daddy quite definitely said—"

"Oh Liss of course there *is*, he's just too vain to admit."

"Well but—"

"Well love if *I* were going to be unfaithful it'd be *with* somebody!"

They both screamed musically with laughter.

"Of course once he's *there*," the friend went on, waving her little bangled wrist for their coffee, "who knows who he'll pick up, your own baby sister told me he has this affetto if not worse for Italian girls."

"*Daddy?*"

"Because Nickie told her your father discusses them in detail with him, pare che sopratutto gli piacciono *Roman* girls, dear, so now you know."

Here, smirking courteously, the maggiordomo bowed low over them pouring their coffee; so for a choice of languages Melissa said more or less in English, "Oh well dear love what Nickie says, ptah."

"No but he might know!"

"No but you know the perfectly possessed things he says! last time I saw him he was 'cultivating un petit air faisandé,' leering; dear he's an adversity!"

"Well Liss he *is* very good-looking. Or in that great gangling way."

"Oh at least he doesn't maunder like my *baby* brother, goodness! *He* did I tell you has just announced to us he's engaged again, 'really' this time, to some child at Radcliffe, poor daddy's having to go up there merely to see! Because of course he isn't, only of course each time one has to make sure in case he is!"

"Yes infantile, no but going *back* Lissa, about your father I mean, dearest your own sister said Nickie said—"

"Well she's mad, Nickie knows *just nothing* about daddy! Some clutching little Italian thing? When he's *fifty*?"

"Now Liss you know how they are."

"But daddy simply wouldn't *notice* outside his own generation! what on earth can my sister— Why for example she knows he didn't even notice Morgan when Morgan was *publicly* mooning at him at her own house-party last year! when I mean it was so dismal even daddy's good manners couldn't have coped if he'd so much as looked at her and seen! So when nothing happened what could happen?"

"But then what *happened*?" her friend implored.

"Oh what d'you think? she languished at him in this quivering schoolchild way the way they do, just pathetic."

"Repulsive, yes."

"*Exactly*, and making these immature excuses all weekend to be near him, following him about to Be Alone with him, well it was sheer girlish *dream* dear, of course I was only there these two nights, because I was sorting out my part of the attic because mummy'd taken *on* so, though what does one do with wedding-presents forever? I mean what does she expect, goodness! and that second night Morgan was as good as out of her mind in my room till *dawn* with these drooping lovelorn details in her despair!"

"Love, how sad."

"Love-how-sad and who doesn't sympathize! only anybody would have thought she was *authentically* in love with daddy, just disgusting!"

"Then this was before she'd got Toby, then."

"Toby, oh ptah."

"Well Toby's huge and rather sweetie *I* thought," her best friend said, yawning delicately.

"Oh in that great helpless *way* sweetie if you like," Melissa conceded, "but then what man isn't? and he was a mere child in officer-school. I mean he just hangs open at Morgan mouthwise, who'd give him a second thought."

"Yes I suppose."

"I don't mean that I didn't still feel this most complete pity-and-terror for her, sleepy as I was. Because adolescence, well goodness. Though this Mrs. Barclay that daddy knows, you know how that generation can be, just seemed terribly *amused* when I told her."

"No now but where was all this."

"Because she said I must realize (love, imagine my *not*!) I must realize that daddy was a perfect old angel, our whole sex was endlessly fetched by him (I ran into her at my fitting, is where) so why not children like Morgan too she said? in any case she said it was practically a family trait in Morgan's family, Morgan's own mother—you know, the composer—was aswoon at him for a year."

"*Morgan's mother!*"

"Well so it seems! and she dedicated a concerto to him, I mean love what one finds out! Though she said of course it wasn't likely Morgan knew about all that, did I happen to know whether she did? this passion her mother had for daddy having been just before Morgan was born."

The friend uttered a scream.

"What, dear?"

"You mean she meant that was a *reason* for not knowing?"

"Not knowing what, dear."

"Why, not *knowing*! because Lissa you don't almost certainly think she must have been rather clearly hinting to you Morgan might be *his own daughter*?"

"*Daddy*'s? love you're deranged, how could she, *all* she said was it seemed to her the sort of thing Morgan might not have been told, didn't I think?—one's mother's hopeless passions, after all! There being no one to tell her, would there be."

"So then you're going to tell Morgan."

"Well because why else d'you think Mrs. Barclay told you all this if not to pass it on, goodness!''

"Well but how could I possibly 'tell' Morgan whatever it is when I don't see what there could be to tell, anyhow it might remind Morgan how she tried to hang herself round his stately old neck in her adolescence when he didn't even notice she was *there*, dear! Rather cruel.''

"No, but Mrs. Barclay must have—"

"Particularly when he just recently sacrificed this whole evening taking her to the Maisonnette *merely* as she knows because I argued him into it to have a little peace and qui—   They saw *you*, dear, by the way! well *dearest* how skulking!'' she suddenly purred.

That one uttered a shrill cry.

At which instantly the huntress swooped: "What my darling? when love I'd never guessed you had this dog for him!'' she sang, bright and innocent of eye.

"Why what can you mean!'' cried her frantic prey.

" 'Mean,' why dearest what could I, why nothing!''

"*No* but—"

"Simply who'd ever thought Patrick fetched you so!''

" 'Fetched'!'' she yelped.

"And no one knows? or not *Sam*, I mean how terribly stealthy you must merely have been!''

"Oh Liss oh what *possibly*?'' babbled the quarry. "Why, for anyone to have noticed, oh *what*, to make you for one second *dream*?''

" 'Notice,' why what can you be remembering,'' exulted Melissa, now smoothly casting down her eyes.

"But for example at some party can you mean?''

"Dearest nothing, why *nowhere*!''

"Or anywhere, oh Lissa *tell me*!'' the lovely stricken thing gibbered on. "You *can't* have thought we ever even looked as if we—   Ahhhh but Lissa Lissa it's been so hard *such an agony* to hide,'' she wailed in self-pity at last; and so on into the long murmuring sweet confessional afternoon: the roster of meetings, of partings, the separations, at routs and balls, in the guilt of clandestine and unaccustomed bars, in milling companies with one's husband sometimes a mere eight inches away in the welcoming din;

the anguishes and inconveniences of adultery (as well as of course its sheer heaven)—this emotion described by among others Sophocles with unusual turbidity of sequence as "unwithstandable; love that in a girl's cheek lies nightlong masked aglow; nor can the immortals flee it, land or sea, or man brief as a day"; for ah Love,

> he that has thee has gone mad.

This, mind you, in sober stilted Attic tragedy!—one place, it might have been confidently supposed, where by convention a woman would sometimes (for short periods; and, it is conceded, artificially) think of other than of love.

All Nicholas Romney was doing was enjoy one hour of peace and quiet himself, the innocent next morning, at the piano, fiddling with a setting for

> What amorous pearl, where Lycid lies,
> Pouts her adornment to his eyes

when of all people his son took it into his carnal young head to ring up for permission to bolt off to Europe not end-of-June as planned but (in ravening pursuit of some sleek child Nicholas had never even heard of) tomorrow!

"Now goddammit Nickie," this responsible father had to roar, "now which one is this!"

". . . . ."

"*What* madman's daughter!"

". . . . ."

"How should I remember what I call 'em, all somebody's daughters, mad or not, aren't they?"

". . . . ."

"Oh."

". . . . ."

"I said, 'oh,' what d'ye want me to say!"

". . . . ."

" 'Tone,' what tone, can't say I used any tone I'm aware of."

"....."

"Remember her perfectly; damned unlikely to forget in fact!"

"....."

"My dear boy *no*, all I meant was—"

"....."

"A *vivid* child I suppose I meant if I meant anything, even rather a high-strung little thing perhaps; 'high-mettled' one might even say; but I assure you—"

"....."

"Now my dear Nickie I'm sure she is!"

"....."

"Why of course she is, temperament's the most natur— "

"....."

"Now see here you mustn't think for one moment that I'd consider a lovely sultry young dancer wasn't perfectly—"

"....."

"What the devil's your mother's remark got to do with it!"

"....."

"Well among other things you did spring her on us pretty abruptly you'll admit! and now here she is just as abruptly back again."

"....."

"I see."

"....."

"Yes but dammit all, months gone by and not a breath out of you about her since."

"....."

"Yes but what about that delicious little Goucher one you've—"

"....."

"Oh *she*'s not going over till *July*; I see!"

"....."

"One in Paris one in Geneva, mm."

"....."

"Oh, three hundred, three hundred twenty-five miles, I suppose you could call it a shuttle if you liked, why not."

"....."

"Except that Nickie my *dearest* boy don't you think two of these highly charged lovely mechanisms at the same time dammit is—"

"....."

"Affairs with two girls simultaneously, you must be out of your senses!"

"....."

"All right all right 'in love with' two simultaneously then: at your age it's a damn' quibble!"

"....."

"All right a quibble at any age!"

"....."

"Now I'm really not prepared to tolerate this irresponsibility of yours d'ye hear? getting into bed with 'em isn't the whole story!"

"....."

"Responsible to her, yes, only by heaven you do seem to feel that about several of the charming little things in a row, don't you!"

"....."

"I mean they want to be *looked after* dammit; what else?"

"....."

"How do I know why they do? simply do."

"....."

"Because if you want to grow up into a 'man who understands women' as you put it, responsible happens to be the absolute first thing you have got to be by god!"

"....."

"Upset, of course they're upset!"

"....."

"Well they haven't *got* anything but undergraduates, if that isn't enough to upset a girl what is?"

So in a word all he was doing, after abusing his dear son, was putter in blameless peace and quiet over a musical setting for

> What amorous pearl, where Lycid lies,
> Pouts her adornment to his eyes,

when his Victoria rang up and intemperately demanded what wickedness was he up to! because this for-years friend, one of her four or five *closest* friends, had seen him of all things irresponsibly dancing at the St. Regis with some sweet little minx or other, what *was* he doing!

He cried out, "Now what's this!" taken aback.

"She *saw* you there!" Mrs. Barclay denounced him. "And in that brummagem Maisonnette or whatever it is!"

"In the what? why dammit I was in the Iridium Room."

"*Where?*"

"Why my angel I was simply off on this new policy of Melissa's," he reasonably besought her. "Now you can't be calling it irresponsible!"

"You took Melissa *dancing*?"

"*God* no, Victoria, merely she suggested the entire—bullied me into it actually, if you care for the blunt fact."

"Nicholas what are you talking about, *what* policy!"

"This policy of Melissa's? why what about it? simply my evenings! said go out on the town now and then as a policy, why not."

"Yes I mean who then was it."

"Now see here my angel, she said the thing was, and I thought after all how sensible, she said why not take out someone unattached I already knew, meaning no involvement d'ye see? Because I mean she *suggested* all this, Victoria! Even more or less, uh, picked the young woman for me as a matter of fact."

"Do you insist I am actually to believe this dementing tale?" she cried in a voice of rage.

"But it's the truth!" he bayed guiltily.

" '*Truth*'!"

"Now surely Victoria you can't seriously—"

"Nicholas are you going to admit the name of this surreptitious girl you had with you or aren't you!"

So he croaked, "Well the fact is it was I suppose Morgan."

Mrs. Barclay appeared to be speechless.

"My utter angel," he began—

"Not that deranged child! you can't mean you've been seeing her!"

"But Melissa sug— "

"*Encouraging* her, Nicholas you must be out of your senses!"

" 'Encourage'! but what frivolous interpretation's this? when you yourself said she and your stepson—"

Mrs. Barclay uttered a little jeweled scream.

"But dammit Victoria fundamentally the child's for all we know merely unoccupied now the young oaf's back at sea again, what more natural."

" 'Child,' 'unoccupied,' oh *really* Nicholas your expressions!"

"But what perverse—"

"And now you'll of course try to conceal the whole guilty performance, oh how unprincipled and graceless you are!" she cried at him.

"Why what is there to conceal, now by god what's suddenly depraved in taking some young woman feeding and dancing?"

"*Dancing*, I've not the slightest doubt the little thing complacently pointed out to you that there she was all evening in your arms!"

Nicholas uttered a cry.

"*And* saw to it that you kissed her the most lingering and murmurous goodnight! Or was there even occasion to say goodnight, did you instead simply— Do you *dare* admit it? Oh where can that dolt that *lout* of a Toby ever have picked up this scheming abandoned knife-wielding little—"

"Victoria will you *listen* to me!" he bellowed.

"*No!*" she screamed at him, and hung up.

She then instantly rang him back. "Nicholas what can your daughter have been even *thinking* of!" she demanded in a passion.

"My angel Vict— "

"Do you have the face to deny it?"

"I was merely—"

"Because Nicholas how can you *treat* me so!" she raved.

"A girl young enough to be my daughter? now what else beyond a little dancing could I pos— "

"*What* else!"

"I tell you I—"

"How often have you seen her again then!"

"Seen Morgan again? what on earth makes you think—"

"Do you realize," Mrs. Barclay told him in tones of menace, "that this is almost *literally* the despicable lying sort of phrase you used to me years ago on another odious occasion? In one of the most wounding scenes your indefensible conduct ever forced me to go through!"

"My angelic creature what is all this even about?" he implored as if unhinged.

"You don't *remember* how you lied?!"

"I—"

"About that horrible little Angelina Hume!" she yelled.

He gaped, stunned.

"I don't suppose I know even yet how often you may or may not have lied to me! And at the very time when we—when I was so—"

"My blessed Victoria—"

"I was *so* in love with you, and I simply went off to Nassau for *ten days* and you took up with her again!"

" 'Took up'!" he gobbled.

"*Slept with* the over-dressed simpering little tart again then, in plain English, oh how could you!" she sniveled, weeping with rage; and *crash*!! went her phone.

Nor this time did she ring him back.

Though he waited long past any reasonable time, gloomily banging the piano (a divertimento called Percussion Sonata For A Pretty Bottom), women being what they alas were.

For how could she! Here were the rooms they'd made love in, the hallways of what greetings, what partings, the oval stair's half-landing too where once— Had she no memory of their love's landscapes? or saw him as he, ah how constantly, saw her, coming toward him along some unforgotten perspective, some Roman street that year, a via, a viale, racing toward him waving perhaps, eyes shining. Or in sunlight on some stone stair, as down from Santa Trinità de' Monti that day, "at the first landing of the elegant stair owly Thomas pray for us," he quoted himself as of some eighteen years earlier, apostrophizing his generation's bard.

Had she no memory? Did she forget their Alpine meadow, deep in spring? and how in those brilliant mornings he waited in the forests' rim above, in the gloom of the hemlocks, waiting when how could a man wait! for her to come climbing the long mountain-meadow from her hotel far below in the blaze of day, up and up and up and up, swaying on her high heels, panting, happy eyes searching the dark thickets for him as she clambered near at last (ah come se ne ricordave!) and then the final gasping laughing rush into his eager arms, and the brown pine-needled forest floor.

Did she now propose to deny all that?

Because by god if she chose to forget there were thank God other women who'd be delighted to remember!—Arabella Hobbes for one! and stamping to the scrutoire he rummaged for the latest of those sporadic letters this sweet Celt from his past still tossed at him now and then from Lyon or Paris or Geneva or wherever any current husband happened to be:

Insufferable Sassenach why do you never arrive where *I* have a milieu? I love you. I love you and I miss you permanently. Sweet pig are you going to let the locks close with me in one continent and you in another? Je t'embrasse fort *fort*.

A.

For then why *not* go abroad at once? ...

They might meet somewhere like (say) the Closerie des Lilas, a visit of piety, purely classical in feeling, to that monument of so many humane generations, including even Henry James. And, meeting *there*, Arabella and he might well feel once more the happy weight of the hours, the sheer total days, they must in all have spent on the breathless scheduling of when they'd manage to see each other next, be in each other's arms, what with that insufferable French husband's comings and goings! the very Closerie where (ah me) that madcap Celt of his had once murmured, dreamily sucking a fingertip, "If we had it all to live over again *darling* Nicholas d'you suppose we'd really go to all this *trouble*?" and collapsed upon him in helpless laughter, in Arcadian un-innocence and joy.

So why not!

So he'd go. Clear up this Radcliffe-child chore of his stupefying son's, and *go*.

He had therefore just bellowed down into the basement to his man to pack him a couple of bags would he? for a night in Boston and have the car brought around right after lunch, when his front door was flung open and there on his threshold was Morgan, little scarlet lip quivering, eyes enormous with outrage and humiliation—who cut the air past him and into the front drawing-room like the swish of a kriss, crashing into a fine light French-walnut chair knocking it sens dessus dessous and caroming off with some fuming little sound, to end up at the long front windows absolutely without a look at him, glaring near-sightedly out at her unpaid taxi or whatever she wanted him to think she *was* glaring at, possibly nothing.

Nicholas collected his wits enough to follow, with a re-assembled smile, informing her shivering little back, in a voice of well-brought-up un-astonishment, that this visit was an agreeable surprise.

She simply sank her head lower, clapped her slim palms over her ears to shut out his loathsome libertine accents, and responded, if response was what it was, with a mewling cry.

He being naturally unable to make anything out of any of this, was fool enough to say so.

At which she spun round upon him, eyes as good as blind with tears, and blazed at him she wondered his unfeeling black heart as much as bothered, why did he even let her cross his doorsill at all!!

Nicholas's jaw opened and hung, a permanency.

"If *that*'s all you think of me I mean!" she cried at him chokingly. And when he gaped on, rushed at him stamping, splashing him and everything around with great topaze tears, "Or do you just *hate* me then, why don't you admit it, you don't even think I'm pretty, you wish I'd never been born don't you!" and baring her little white teeth at him, "*Italian girls!*" she screeched, and fled wildly into the back drawing-room, where she flung herself onto the piano-bench and set about shattering the air with volley after volley of horrible treble chords.

Nicholas followed, wincing.

"*And don't touch me!*" she instantly bleated, and sprang up and scuttled round into the stair-hall, "I will *not* be soothed and got around and patted patted patted patted, I loathe the very touch of you," she babbled, rushing through the hall and around into the front drawing-room again, "how would you feel if *I* only pretended you attracted me, oh how stupid how gullible you'd be, oh how I despise you! Oh how can you *bear* to just stand there and disgust me so!" she squalled, and fled into the hall again and up the stairs and into his bedroom, where she plunged face-down into his great bed, howling.

What could he do but follow? and stand there glaring down at her, speechless, as she wallowed and hiccupped!

So she at once demanded in a muffled shriek *must* he stand there staring at her agony, gloating over how he had made her weep till she looked hideous? so he'd have an excuse for never looking at her disfigured as she was again!

He essayed a tentative there there, in a resigned fashion. To which she responded with moans of hatred and misery.

Presently, in a gingerly way, he risked sitting down by her, a position on which she immediately turned her delightful little back, punching and biting into his pillows and showering him with still more fragments of sob-mangled rodomontade, "Because you never liked me, not once in all that time, every sweet thing you ever said to me was a heartless lie, even letting me think I interested you and *pleased* you" and so forth; anybody can reconstruct the sort of thing. But when he thereupon proceeded to the routine next stage of mildly patting her shoulder, up she jumped and ran round the bed ranting, and round the room and into the bathroom and out, and did he for one instant fancy in his great smug oaf of a heart that she hadn't lied to him too? for what else could she do when he treated her so! how could anyone treat anyone so! "even if you loathed everything I ever did to try to please you how *could* you treat— Oh Nicholas Nicholas Nicholas I am so lost so slain!" she ended, casting herself contentedly weeping into his completely apprehensive arms.

So this went on.

It took in fact no less than half an hour of what was left of the whole outrageous morning by god just to draw enough cold water to wash her tear-blackened little face!

Then, she felt so faint there was a question whether she didn't need a brandy instantly, so he was sent shambling off for that while she lay weak and lovely in a slipper chair, but when he got back with the stuff she felt enough better *not* to need it, he was sweet to fetch it but she reminded him he might perfectly well have remembered she *dis*liked brandy, detailing to him two occasions at his own baby daughter's house-party when, in his very presence, she had refused it. Or else he had noticed but simply didn't care.

After that he was sent off so she could do her face.

But if he had nothing else to do while she *did* her face, he might for example fetch a fresh pillow-case before the maid (or whoever) came and found *this* lipstick-smeared rag, which (she sweetly cooed at him) looked as if she'd gnawed it in the most heavenly transports while he was having his beastly will with her.

So he went to the linen-closet looking. But she also immediately called that she'd left her bag with lipstick and compact in it *naturally* downstairs it would be right under his nose, how could anybody miss it? so he went down and rummaged about and brought it. Also got her two more clean towels, and a box of kleenex. And a box of that fluffed cotton. And went down and paid off her taxi.

No sooner back in the house though, and sunk in a chair in the drawing-room to wait, than sure enough he heard her crying again. So he heaved himself to his feet and trundled up for the whateverth time. But now all she broken-heartedly wanted was for him to forgive her. For how could she have subjected him to all that? and so on—the whole smothered rhetoric of contrition, nose buried in his lapel and her arms quivering round as much of his big torso as she felt she might humbly move in on, lifting at last a wet but peaceful face, which inevitably he kissed; and so on round to cold-water compresses again.

Though would he please *stay* this time because there was something she would almost certainly want to say to him before she did her face.

This turned out to be an appeasing complaint: "I *know* I said things I shouldn't 've, Nicholas, but there is one thing I bet you didn't notice as much as you would have if I'd ever got you to behaving the way I want to me."

"Is, huh!" the man more or less snarled.

"See? you didn't notice at all!"

He smouldered at her, speechless.

"Or I suppose it's perfectly pointless to ask," she said in now meek tones, "whether you ever think about any of the things you might guess I do because of you, *for* you. When you didn't even notice."

"Notice *what*!"

"Why should I even tell you! All you do is humiliate me!"

" '*All* I do'!"

"You said to that red-faced man with the dirty stock— Oh how can I admit everything to you! Oh well damn damn, you know it anyway, I have no pride with you! So I do have to hate you sometimes, so there! so I heard you say to him in the paddock why aren't American women woman enough to admit the necessity of high heels and my heart utterly foundered and that night I crept out and threw two pairs of shoes that hadn't absolutely *spike* heels under the first culvert down the carriage-drive. Because my legs *are* nice," she finished, thrusting them out from the bed in sleek display.

Delicious, he gruffly admitted.

She turned them on their high heels in gentle gourmandise, saying, "From any angle, too."

"Well, damn' pretty legs evidently!" he exclaimed, nervous.

But she mourned, "Oh I always have to prompt you so!"

"Now my sweet child, look, a man of my age can't just—"

She leaped to her feet and shrieked at him *stop* saying such things, age age age age age *age*, he maddened her with it, he said it *only* to madden her, to shatter her with frustration! and she ran round the room chattering like a little demon what had his *age* to do with it, hadn't she wanted him the minute she'd laid eyes on him? was it age that kept him from simply stretching out his hand and taking her, sick with love as he *perfectly well* knew she was? or was it his hideous archaic standards of conduct instead! his hateful victorianism or whenever he'd been born, leaving her in this fever of longing and submission and shame, "or are you going to pretend you didn't want me too at least that one morning as much as I wanted you?" she gasped in pain.

Nicholas gaped at this roommate of his own baby daughter's drop-jawed and speechless again.

"Ah but it was so sweet so *sweet*," she wept, crumpling in self-pity into the nearest chair. "My one pitiful threadbare memory of you," she sniffled, forlorn; and collapsed still further, this time to the floor, where she sank effortlessly into the lines of ultimate classic despair. "I crept into your room," she said in a voice so low that no first-row balcony could have caught a word of it, "oh it was barely dawn; so dewy, so cool; so hushed; there was no one in the world but you and me, and there you lay huge and sprawled, and oh Nicholas—"

He bellowed, "By god you know as well as I do I thought you were some confounded daughter come to pester me awake!"

"You patted my shoulder, and then your hand—"

"Different hair-do, damn' unexpected shock if you care to know it!" he cried at her.

"Then you opened your eyes and looked at me in that lovely pallid light and I sat there and oh no woman ever in your bed was more tenderly and strickenly yours my dearest, ah I could see everything you were thinking, your eyes were so near, all sorts of shining floating expressions, and I in this utter sweet terror and determination; and then suddenly you asked me in that *therapeutic* tone if I was all right, and I was so—I was so— Well what *could* I say damn you!" she shrieked, on her feet again, stamping at him, "when all the *matter* was I wanted to get into your bed only you looked as if you'd fling me straight out the window, wouldn't you 've, bully and brute that you are, you *would* have too!" she sobbed. And hurled herself into the bathroom and violently locked the door, and started splashing cold water all over again.

So he went downstairs.

And sat, shaken.

Because all very well to say learned his lesson, but *what* lesson! When why *not* "stretch out his hand and take"? Was he after all these years changing his goddam spots?

Got to his feet and paced from front drawing-room to back drawing-room, and glared at his watch; then front again and glared at the Copley, and if he was changing then why squat here in a palaeolithic stew merely because this wild little beauty of his lacked a certain reserve?

When what was it anyhow but a pure matter of female style: merely she hadn't the usual billowy decorum!

So then a touch of tolerance dammit! At his age he could afford to! Or when forced to, anyhow!

This little Cartesian review, in fact, presented the state of affairs not only without the scrabbling about and the discomfort but with many of the stately appas of pure reason thrown in; so by the time his young lady finally came tripping down, all sweet and self-possessed once more, he could ungruffly remark time had sort of got *on* what with this and that hadn't it! and urge her why not stay take lunch with him wouldn't she? in the sunny brilliance of the garden and all? short notice of course but considering the hour? actually a minor meal, just a cold soup, a crème de concombre he thought it was, then a suprême de volaille, and a salad to glisten in the noon light. He'd also had the man add a little crêpe farcie to help keep body and soul together, glazed crêpes actually and very pretty with their glossy little crests of sliced and lozenged truffles; and though for dessert he couldn't offer her fraises des bois he was afraid, still there was this bavarois with kirsch-soaked strawberries piled round in crimson dunes; and the man had a Montrachet flashing green and gold in its ice.

She said with a sweet look at him that she'd love to.

"Because dammit," he hurried on, "this outlandish whatever-it-is, relationship, hardly know what, between you and me—total absence of any term from the language if you want my opinion! And I include Freudian technicalities!" he ended with violence. "Now dammit can't I get you a sherry?" he in part shouted, springing up again.

This, eyes cast down, she meekly accepted.

"The thing is, to take these things *calmly*, in the name of heaven!" he made her see.

She murmured the most docile assent, and sipped.

"In a word, my lovely little thing, you and I do really have to get our, huh, our mutual history into some sort of handle-able order my god!"

"But then Nicholas this was exactly my plan."

".....uh?"

"Oh but surely this morning you can't—"

"I mean once for all, hope you *see* that!"

"Well of course, only *not* now, when I do think my dearest you might spare me that now of all moments."

"How's that?" he cried hollowly.

"Why, when you've just put me through such hell over you, I mean all morning long!"

"When *I*'ve just—!"

"Well when anyway you won't dare say I haven't been *through* it! Because how in any case could I possibly suffer like this if it weren't for you, my darling? Or are you going to wound me still more by some cruel unfeeling pretence that you don't believe I do suffer?"

"*Dammit* Morgan—"

"In fact I don't see how you could ever have brought yourself to suggest it," she reproached him in a voice full of pain. "And Nicholas we do have all the time in the world really. I mean for explanations. So, my dearest, I forgive you after all."

He started to say, "Now Morgan I want you to realize I don't even—"

But "Now do we have to just suffocate in here with that lovely sunny glowing little walled garden to wait for lunch in instead?" she sang to him, springing lightly up and stepping with a click of high heels toward the garden doorway, where she paused waiting, great eyes wide and softly upon him until (for what else could he do?) he'd got up and tagged along and come up with her, whereupon she took one step and stood against his heart, lifting her mouth to say now couldn't she just once be kissed? without fussing? just, very sweetly, once?

So therefore.

Then they went out, and shortly had lunch. To which he had the man add a goat-cheese.

He was therefore later than planned leaving for Boston after lunch, in fact a quarter to five.

And with no especial moral to point, either, as he wove northward through the glowing green and gold of early-summer-evening countryside; none that is that a man of brains need bother about. What was this business of homilies anyhow but mankind's fatuous and age-old yearning for the Book of Answers! There never had been answers; never would be; merely a linguistic mistake of Greek philosophy's we'd taken over, that if the word existed the thing it denoted existed too. Why, the only serious desiderata for a normal Indo-European are a pretty girl within grabbing range, a dazing drink, and somebody to knock down.

Hymns of self-praise or self-pity on these topics are standard too, being in fact our literature. But answers, no. So he sang

> What call ye this?—my fausse, my fair,
> My gilded honey says me nay

most of the way to the Connecticut line.

Answers he would admit would be very cosy: if everybody could for example find out how everybody else felt, by running one of these beef-witted opinion-surveys on it, then everybody might temporarily be less uneasy about how they felt themselves.

Or again, answers filled up space very decoratively if one had nothing urgent to say about what was actually going on: he'd instance what's-his-name from his own generation, Eliot, that Pindar of the prie-dieu, *wonderfully* lyric and readable on there's-nothing-to-be-done-about-anything. Well, there never had been, but was that a reason for inventing answers saying there had?

This warm and lovely little Morgan and her psychiatrist merely for one example: ah, what irresponsibility. Or else what haunting ignorance. And what a conception of Man! for fancy "happiness" as a goal for a being whose immemorial ambience is catastrophe! Here we'd been, since the dawn of history, stumbling onward and upward, as if that were the right direction, dodging the endless thunderbolts (le bon Dieu, si archaïsant) and now here came psychiatry to "adjust" us to being knocked sprawling! Did they seriously conceive of Achilles or for variety Michelangelo being "happy"? Why, in this badly lighted world we take one pratfall after another over whatever it is props up the scenery, complaining of our contusions and abrasions and denouncing the inconveniences, and this is normal and understood; and moreover (as just said) is all literature.

> Ahi, nel dolore nasce
> L'Italo canto

and who'll say what mightn't have become of the unobliterated spirit of man if they'd been able to rid Michelangelo of his "conflicts" by god, or applied group-therapy to the tantrums of Achilles!

The immediate problem wasn't Morgan however or for that

matter mankind, but he *did* have to compose a little note to be sent round by messenger to this daughter-in-law, if that was what for once it'd turn out to be, at Radcliffe.

Who presented herself in polite wonder at his Cambridge hotel mid-morning next day, a sleek little golden thing in Bermuda shorts and a boy's shirt, feet moreover in sneakers, and as feared not only didn't consider herself in the least engaged to his huge infant of a younger son but visibly didn't even really remember what boy this might be.

This gaping hole in the amenities they both rushed, shaken, to fill, in something of an excess of hasty good manners—he expressing the profuse hope that she'd take dinner with him that very evening, bestow *that* pleasure on him anyhow if only as salvage from this, huh, this rather misled little encounter, and she simultaneously producing the most melting look to beg him come with *her* to this lecture she had to go to this next hour on Book 30 of the Paradiso, because there was *just* time for them to make it if they went at once and this professor was brilliant, he was *brilliant*, and if Mr. Romney was a Princeton man he'd probably never in his life been to an intellectual Harvard lecture had he, how sad how deprived-sounding, so it would be an Experience. Thus seemliness was retrieved, he saying that this suggestion of hers delighted him, and she, of his dinner, that she would adore it.

The lecture, reversing accepted academic methodology, illumined Dante by special insights into Kierkegaard, the suovetaurilia, Fermi, Braque, Keynes, Peter the Great, and the geography of Dublin.

His dolce dottore then very civilly walked him back to his hotel. Where, as the first thing to catch his eye was Mrs. Barclay's Daimler glittering at the curb, he made his adieux outside.

Mrs. Barclay however was in his sitting-room. Why, *here* he was (she said in tones of pardon) where on earth had he been? because she was on her way to Concord to see the headmaster over something she needn't go into, a very minor contretemps and in any case what did they expect? fifth-formers being what they were, and she just happened to have rung up his house in a chance and idle moment before she left New York, chiefly to say perhaps she should not have rung off so brusquely as to have deprived him of the chance to express the regrets he might well have been suffering from ever since (she now saw) for his conduct toward her. So that was how by pure accident she'd found out where he'd run off to. So *that* was how she'd decided, since she was making this trip to Concord in any case, to break it at Cambridge and show her willingness to forgive him by letting him feed her lunch. So that he could explain.

After this they went amiably down to the dining-room, where, once he'd ordered, he began describing his dilemma, for as she knew he obeyed her lightest word of command, yet in what terms could a Platonic evening be "explained" to her? other than as Platonic.

"Now really Nicholas," she said reasonably, "will you maintain that a word like 'Platonic' is even in character?"

"But when I keep swearing to you—"

"Now for example what tone do you use with this girl of my poor stepson's, what do you talk about."

"Talk about, how can *I* remember!"

"You mean you don't propose to tell me?"

"Dammit Victoria you know as well as I do I can't remember conversations; never did!"

"You can't recall one single thing she's said to you?" Mrs. Barclay charged.

"Now as it happens I can! Why, it was an outrageous thing, too!"

"Something *she* said to you was?"

"Yes; now this place was packed d'ye see, no agreeable sense of space the way it was in the Thirties, Victoria, dammy if I'm sure it's even the same room, *done* something to it somehow, and in this swaying mob Morgan suddenly spotted of all people Melissa's college roommate."

"Who?"

"Don't remember her married name, but if you'll credit this

there she quite openly was with some young whelp she's by heaven having an affair with, Morgan informed me! She *told* me this!'' he fulminated, and fell dismally silent.

So she had to urge him, ''Yes, so in what sense then?''

''Ahn?''

''I mean so then what.''

''*That* doesn't strike you as enough?''

''No I mean the *point* of this story Nicholas.''

''I said it wasn't young Sam with her! Wasn't the wretched girl's husband, it's some disconcerting damn' affair!''

''Well but Nicholas young people *do*.''

He said glumly, ''But dammit Victoria *Melissa*'s roommate!''

''Now you can't forget *I* was married when I fell in love with you!'' she cried.

''No but can't you see it's startling, Victoria,'' he argued, pouring the wine, which he then tasted with sceptical grimaces, ''to find the extent of what I hadn't even suspected about my own daughter?''

Mrs. Barclay said in an augmented tone, ''But it's not your precious Melissa who's having this miserable affair!''

''Victoria be sensible, what I mean is here's this standard little urban amour not merely ventilated with the maddest romanticism in my baby daughter's circle mind you, but by heaven it's her best friend!''

''Nicholas of *all* tiresome misplaced—''

''My own sweet daughter by god and I'm at a loss to understand even the elements of her comportment!''

Mrs. Barclay emptied her glass in irritation and told him he knew *perfectly* well!

''All the same it makes me damned uneasy if you want to know,'' he mumbled.

''So then what did this bewitching child say to you next about this,'' she prompted him.

''Uh? what child's this?''

''This chattering little Morgan whatever's-her-name, you know perfectly *well* who I mean!'' she cried piercingly. ''And how can you bear to be so transparent, well go on go on why won't you go *on!*'' she accused him, though all he was doing was attentively refill her glass.

"Well, about this generation? or how d'you mean."

"Your irresponsible conduct with this devious child, what else could I possibly mean!"

So in sheer defense he rambled into an analysis: "Now my lovely Victoria what's this everlasting 'irresponsible'? merest routine good manners to let a woman feel she's a woman surely, what other course's conceivable! I grant a woman adores this sometimes to the point of thinking she adores the man too; but if this happens to convince the giddy thing she has to acquire him as well, poor devil how's that *his* fault? Then when he declines to break his accommodating neck undertaking this responsibility, in other words to acquire *her* by god permanently, she shrieks at him how irresponsible he is!"

"So then this is what this clandestine little thing's been giving you to understand!"

"Uh?"

"That she adores you, what else!" Mrs. Barclay denounced him in a glittering voice.

"Now my reasonable angel you can't be maintaining—"

"It's *disgustingly* clear!"

"But Victoria—"

"And what am *I* to do about you? when you behave like this with one maladjusted clinging child after another!" she fumed.

So he was driven to telling her in manly declamation, "You might *trust* me then for once by almighty heaven!" open and honest as daylight—for where were there a woman and man on earth with a remembered history like theirs? and hadn't he told her and told her?—how happily, how constantly, his memory saw her coming to meet him, toward him, *to* him, out of that unfading past, through the warm noons of Roman streets, the splash of fountains, or she was in sunlight on some broad marble stair, arms full of flowers, descending, coming to him, *his*—and now she spoke as if none of this had ever been, he said heavily.

And refilled their glasses, sighing.

While she sat with lovely eyes cast down.

For what he asked did she conceive love to be if not this continuum, the present what it was because of what was before? why otherwise should he remind her of what lay in memory between them? for didn't she, as he, remember their Alpine meadow deep in spring—

"I should never have had anything to do with you, ah Nicholas," she lamented tenderly.

"You're shaking inside this minute as you did then, admit you are!"

This, eyes deep in his, she mistily pronounced simply untrue.

"Shaking like a sheer girl!" he exulted, making a happy grab for her hand.

"Ah Nicholas what wild conceit."

"But you are, you lovely unforgetting—"

"I am not, oh darling, no," she breathed.

"*I*'m shaking, just at seeing you for this mere—"

But she said, "You'd just had your hair cut," as in dream.

"I'd *what*?"

"Hair cut, oh Nicholas think," she mourned.

"Now when was this, why what an endlessly sweet thing to have remembered somehow!"

"Well you *had*. When naturally I remember how you looked."

"All I meant—"

"And when the way you looked was that you *had* just had your hair cut why should I remember you as having it long? When it was short."

"Why, I suppose so!" he cried, amazed.

"Oh cuore mio *remember*?"

So they gazed at each other through a haze of angels. She murmured, "Must go, caro," in virgin revery, "darling literally fly," not stirring.

"Now how could I ever let you go!"

"Or want to, ah sweet," she sighed, eyes drifting to their entwined contented hands.

But as he was triumphantly announcing, "Then angel stay!" the maître d'hôtel bowed over them, madam's chauffeur having sent in word, as madam had instructed, to remind madam that madam had wished to set out at two.

They stared at each other dashed, beset.

In anguish or in outrage, "My angel then will you dammit come to dinner tomorrow, you never come visit me!" he charged.

"Ah Nicholas I know I've been neglecting you," she lied to him in tenderest penitence.

"So then come on then!"

"For example I haven't even come by to make sure you're comfortably settled, have I."

"How's that?" he cried out.

"Really looked after and *cared* for you Nicholas darling, I should keep seeing to it!"

"Then will you come to dinner?"

"*Tomorrow?*"

"Or day after then?"

"Oh *how* miserable, when dinners, oh Nicholas you might very well guess how impos— "

"*Lunch* then day after tomorrow, dammit my lovely Victoria now say you will!"

"Well possibly lunch the day after *that* was what I actually had in mind," she confessed in a voice now as smooth as cream, neither of them needing (at their age) to be so insensible as even to remember that this would be the man's day off.

So that evening he could light-heartedly feed the Radcliffe child (who, it turned out at considerable length at dinner, had thought of doing her junior paper on Bramante's early Milanese period but the subject was *so* broad) and deliver her punctually at this 8:30 seminar she had on Kepler; thus he was back in his sitting-room in the hotel, yawning pleasurably and on the point of bed in good time for once, in fact only waiting for the radio to finish off one of Bach's everlasting ethereal variations on the Sailor's Hornpipe, when of all possible things the door opened and there was Morgan.

Looking this time like a somber and sulky little thundercloud and muttering, "Well I am just desperate Nicholas so there!" before she'd even lifted her haunted face to be kissed.

Indeed hardly kissed him at all before she was fretting, "I know it's all very convenient and comfortable for *you* Nicholas, but you might realize *I* had to cut a rehearsal to come here after you. And I'd never see you if I didn't!" she concluded peevishly, rebuking him still further by not only not kissing him again but in fact taking herself ungraciously right out of his arms.

And in a pet flicked the radio from Bach to some young woman who sang in a voice of sugary delinquency "wunna be bad rill baaad" before Nicholas could leap snarling and snap the thing off.

Morgan immediately said, "Well Nicholas I know I shouldn't be furious with you but it *is* your fault that I'm so worried now about Toby that I'm in this unending sleepless anguish over it! So *of course* I had to come discuss it with you!"

'*His* fault'!

"Well my dearest it *is*, why, you brought it all up, you *reproved* me for not thinking about Toby when I'm engaged to him and now I *keep* thinking about it, oh how could you!" she chattered, eyes filling with tears.

He started to say he was blest if he saw offhand what pos—

"So naturally I had to follow you then!" she cried in indignation. "Because when I'm so complex who else understands me, my darling? Not that you do—*oh* you can be so blind! But I mean you do at least partly know how utterly—oh Nicholas how *enslavedly* I seem to love you! because truly don't you?" she pleaded, coming to him.

He patted her, and declared with a belated lightness of tone that he wasn't so insensible as to deny she'd had the flattering good manners to make it plain she felt so.

"Oh well when I couldn't help myself as you know perfectly well; but I mean what would Toby *do* is what I want you to explain, is why I came. I mean would he get special leave d'you think or something equally desperate?"

Nothing desperate about a leave! what if he did?

" 'Nothing desperate'!" she echoed, almost in a shriek. "When only yesterday Melissa for example told me her own best friend asked her whether she thought Sam might even kill her if he found out about Patrick? and Melissa says she *just doesn't know*!" she whispered in horror.

He said now what staring nonsense was this! did her generation take its coups de théâtre from the tabloids?

But she said, "Yes only what will Toby *do*? oh Nicholas how does any woman ever find out what goes on in your heads, the way you plunge wildly past and all."

He said these Yale boys, ptuh, needn't worry her pretty head about 'em, nothing against Toby personally of course but Yale boys like the Victorians always thought up was *up*.

"Well Nicholas what difference does it make where you went to college, but you *have* to warn me what he may do, can't you see?" she implored him. "Because you are responsible for me, Nicholas!"

Now look, he said humanely, now couldn't she realize? her enchanting sex had been saying *Look at me, dance with me* and the like to him ever since he could remember, and that was the whole damn' trouble.

"Oh I know I'm not a new experience to you, you don't have to remind me!" she said with a gasp, drooping, delivering herself instantly from his arms. "I know you're a libertine, my psychiatrist says so, anyway I know you won't ever love me, love *deeply* Nicholas, the way I love you, it's just not in your nature I guess," she said in a low tone, blinking rapidly. "Which you know *is* why she keeps saying there's no happy future for me in loving you. Oh as if I cared! Or as if living without you could seem a 'future' to me, my darling, even if it stretched out till I'm a hundred. Oh but Nicholas she does have my good at heart though," she fretted all woe-begone, "even saying you're bad for me."

He said with some natural heat the woman was a fool, *he* 'bad for her'!

"Yes but the *worst* is, she tries to make me think I'm bad for you too, I can't bear it!"

Not good for him? what, when here she was caressing his advancing years with this sweetest blandishment, this most touching of all flatteries, her young beauty's devotion?

"Oh oh please not about *age* my dearest!" she mourned. "Oh you understand women so little—*so little*!—when you talk about age like that!" she half-wept in exasperation and despondency.

"I'd love you when you were eighty—*will* love you when!" she wailed, starting up, confronting him.

Long before *that* unaccommodating milestone, he said soberly, he hoped some honest old friend would have the common humanity to put him down.

"Oh but Nicholas this *isn't* just that I'm young and in love, *terribly* in love, for the first time, can't you see that? Have I ever said I wasn't young and inexperienced? Or can't you admit that even though I am, you still could be the one love of my life? Because you are! and why couldn't my first love be my real one!"

He said, well, in principle—

"So I can't even *make* my mind think about Toby, oh I just don't love him at all," she moaned in loveliest distraction. "Because oh even you must see I have a duty to myself, women just *do* I don't care what you say, am I to be irresponsible and deny my love for you? only when I write and tell Toby I'm your mistress he may *kill* himself, my dearest, and then I'll be haunted, oh Nicholas what shall I even do?" she babbled, clinging to him.

He got enough of his thunderstruck voice back to expostulate now now now now, why she must be out of her sweet little female bedlamite mind!! did she suppose at *his* age he'd be so insensible, or her own word "irresponsible" dammit, as to disseize a perfectly decent boy, no matter how hulking, of a girl he—

"Oh how can you misunderstand me so, *hurt* me so!" she choked, through a tide of tears. "As if I'd ever more than glanced— As if what I feel for you could be compared— Well what if I did for one mere moment consider marrying Toby and say I would, was it for anything but to be connected with you? once I'd found out his step-mother is this old family friend so you couldn't just have overlooked me any more the way you'd like to," she ran wretchedly on, tears now showering, "when besides I'd at least have been *seeing* you, Nicholas, not often perhaps but still often, so your image would always have been there under my eyelids, every day fresh and renewed and new, how can you not understand!"

Would she let him finish a sentence? because he was *perfectly* willing to concede her psychiatrist's shooing her back toward Toby was not merely misplaced but a piece of damned imbecility, fancy telling a girl who was in love with one man that she ought to fall in love with another man instead! Nevertheless—

"I never even suspected what love was till I loved you!"

Nevertheless dammit—

"This half-unbearable joy, oh this certainty that I'd found the one being I was created for," she recited softly, as if a quotation, "after my whole lifetime of just ordinary boys and men, my dearest!"

So he sat down, sighing; and started out to suggest that perhaps she hadn't entirely—

"As if till now I'd always lived in some deep hopeless night but now suddenly there is this lovely light of day over everything everywhere, ah can't you see how I must feel at last?"

He said well, yes; because he supposed poetry for example was something anybody wrote till age twenty-five and then gave up (or of course in some cases went on writing, with more studied enigma to it but no less dull) and he wondered whether just as poetry was a kind of first-love of language, so this feeling of hers—

"Well but you *are* the only man I've ever loved, Nicholas," she told him, coming to kneel in front of him before he could scramble up from where he was sitting (which unfortunately was a mock-Empire sofa as big as a bed made for love) and leaning toward him so that he had at all hazards to gaze straight into the child's eyes if only to keep from looking down her dress.

He said well she was a sweet temptress, by god she was; and damn' well she knew it, too, he added, patting her; but now couldn't she all the same recognize the sort of situation—because wasn't it?—that she and he and everybody they knew had been raised *not* to—

"Oh but Nicholas that was only before I'd given *up* Toby, can't you see? when now there's nobody!"

He let out some vacuous unhappy sound as if he no longer had any really workable notion of what this might even mean.

"Because all I have to do is sit down and write to him right now to tell him, and prove to you; and then even you will have to admit, oh my dearest then I *will* be yours!"

He pronounced her name a couple of times over, as if it were in some sheer foreign language.

She said in a choking whisper, "And so then *not* have to wait oh please please after all these endless months any longer my darling?" and stretched blissfully up to be kissed and taken, saying his name as silkily as if she were already swooning enravished in his bed.

Poor devil he besought her now *look* in heaven's reasonable name! wouldn't she like the lovely thing she was merely *listen* to him for ten consecutive seconds for once? for even assuming as the last hypothesis conceivable, the *purest* of absolute assumptions, suppose he did for one putative bewildering minute happen to want her as much as she wanted him—

She said in her throat, "*You do.*"

By god he gobbled if he was going to kiss her be damned if it'd be in *this* preposterous squat, would she stand *up*? scrambling to his feet and hauling her up with him; but then instead of kissing the lovely pleading child like a man in his right mind, he took her determinedly by the shoulders as if possibly to shake her and launched into a homily on (of all topics) maturity.

So naturally she broke in: "But can't you see with your own eyes how loving you has turned me into a woman at last, my dearest?"

Now he *assured* her—

"You think I'm *not*!" she cried, going white.

He said he simply—

"Only then I'm *not*!" she choked, springing away from him. "Oh how can you taunt me so cruelly!" and fled to the sofa, on which she dropped, gasping.

But when he more or less flabbergasted came after her with the ready assuasive rhetoric of solace (or whatever *was* needed) she sprang up in his face squalling "Well then I'm a *virgin* if you must make me tell you damn you!" in mortification and rage, and catapulted past him into the dark bedroom, and banged and bolted the door.

Nicholas slumped back onto the sofa, looking his glummest. And, presently, yawning.

Then, as the silence went on, he stood for a time staring in vacancy and depression out the window onto the nighted street. And went back and sat down again; and almost dozed.

For a long time there was silence. But at last he heard her unbolt and open the door, and then her hand came around the door-jamb and found the switch and turned out the lights. But when in the dimness he went solicitously toward her she slipped past him and stood in the deeper dusk by the doorway to the hall.

Where then she mumbled something in a tone so low that he had to go right up to her to make out what it was.

She whispered with her little back to him that he must not look at her, she was hideous with tears, she knew she was hideous, she'd cried so long and so hopelessly, in her misery, in (for why should she not say it?) her final despair.

He said gently *not* despair, now what sort of Regency performance was this? when here she was with every prospect, with every bright hope.

But she said how could he call it a "performance" when it was just that she loved him, it *was* love, this was what love was, and she murmured an alexandrine which it struck him must be Racine; she loved him and she did not see how he could expect her to just stop. But if it would please him she would try to stop throwing herself humiliatingly at him, if that would make him feel less harassed, for would it? for then she would try, she finished softly, and opened the door.

And as she stepped through said in a sad little voice, "Because Nicholas this *shows* I am grown up. I can Renounce you." And with gentle dignity went down the hall away.

◄§§►

So he had to drive back to New York next morning talking to himself in bafflement and inhibition.

For responsible responsible, who knew what it meant anyhow? flung in his face morning noon and night like this!

As if a man's soul were there to be yelled at!

The soul is a private affair, even the religious bureaucrats were beginning to admit it without all these threats of documented hellfire; le bon Dieu had had better sense all along, and he remembered once in his boyhood his father leaping from the stanhope in a towering passion—they'd been on the road to Peirce's Mills, up a branch of the Black Brandywine, getting a hunter used to driving harness—his father had leaped down and ripped off a pious posted sign

> SIN AND YOU'LL FIND OUT

which he'd beaten to flinders on a stump, roaring *he*'d keep their impertinent yatter out of Chester County for 'em by god! and his father had been *right* by god, no birthright Philadelphia Quaker ever bothered his head over their slave-class preoccupation with the safety of their unappetizing souls, what was this anyhow, the whingeing hagiolatrous tenth century all over again?

—Except of course it was not, admittedly, an answer to much of anything about this sweet little Morgan of his.

Why did this generation suffer so drearily? Where was the styled and handsome anguish of tradition? the whole ravishing diapason, from Edwardian vapors to those wonderful screeching bosom-beating Mediterranean tantrums, how decorative, how in keeping!

Whereas in this present desolate ambience— Why, for instance, for sheer contrast that phrase of Paris's to Helen, in the Iliad, when he can hardly wait for her to get her clothes off, *glukus hímeros hairei*, he pronounced in his mind, *"sweet* desire," could one imagine any intellectually fashionable novelist these days, of any of the four contemporary sexes, calling desire sweet? by heaven they talked as if the only similitude for love were the terminal agonies of cancer!

So in the end he drove into New York lustily singing

> Almighty Sir, of Whose my soul
> An ancient indecision is,

an undergraduate pastiche the prosody of which, and the syntax, still pleased him.

What he'd first thought of feeding his Victoria was an early-summer lunch out of Paul Reboux: a cool gazpacho, then a little glazed crème de cervelle (which, as he wouldn't inform her was cervelle, she'd love), followed by a fine pink-fleshed lake-trout garnished in two shades of green, viz., artichoke hearts and green mayonnaise, and end with a vanilla ice gleaming with slivers of almond and slivers of truffles. But then he remembered she made a tiresome fuss at truffles, which she held were not merely over-rated but rubbery, so after trying in vain to find fraises des bois he had just this cherry tart with a crème aux marrons piped onto it in rococo swags.

That then was what she arrived looking lovely to eat.

He'd laid the table out under the lace-shadowed locust tree in his little walled garden, and almost at once as they ate (she'd barely finished her crème de cervelle—what *was* this delicious thing, a mousse de viande? he said yes) almost at once she said she was concerned over how he proposed to occupy his time once he was in Europe, would he merely like all bankers go to Geneva? because he'd spoken of writing his memoirs or had he really meant a novel, which was what everybody seemed to write instead, and in either case she'd have expected him to go to Paris where he'd always said August and September were his favorite months, with that heavenly golden haze over the Seine in the mornings and enough of everybody away en vacances to make the lovely city seem nearly deserted, for example that time he and she had had the whole Place St. Sulpice to themselves, such a blessing, did he remember? so if he was going to write something, or even set his songs, was Paris possibly where he planned to go and perhaps stay?

So he replied, taking their empty ramekins down and in, to the little back-basement kitchen, and bringing out the glistening trout, on seeing which she cried out how magnificently handsome (as it was), he replied hardly memoirs but now would she notice this Montrachet particularly? because this was a Tastevin bottling which he'd never found before outside of France, he'd come on it only last week uptown, a sheer trouvaille.

Oh *wasn't* it, she exclaimed, sipping, and then with a little sound of delight sipping again, how *really* delectable, he must not just tell her where he'd got it but remind her later too, but did he then mean he remembered that Place St. Sulpice day, what they'd done?

He said with a snort he was aware of this female dogma that men have no memory, even of love, but she didn't seriously expect him to forget the priest her conduct had upset? the suggestion was mere coquetry. No memoirs, no; who'd read a banker's memoirs; and what could he call it if he did, A Short Wait For The Butcher or what? holding up his glass to gaze at the green gold of the wine against the brilliance of early afternoon.

Well then she said he meant he'd be in Paris in for example August?

All August probably; why not.

Because she said she'd asked because she herself might very easily be in Paris too in August for a day or so, anyhow she was not going to follow her husband to Geneva, so this was why she'd wondered about Paris and accordingly asked him; namely because of this possibility she was describing; of being there herself; she meant in August.

To this he naturally if prematurely replied, dropping knife and fork in delight, thank God was she really about to make up her mind about him then, angel that she was?

She cried out in petulance what an utterly wicked lying thing even to say!

So he served her again to trout, dashed.

Which she forgave his indiscretion enough to eat. And launched next into a reporting, or anyhow a selective report, which she contrived to make sound very much like an accounting to him alone, of her life for the period he'd deserted her in, that space of seventeen years which he'd spent she had no way of ever knowing how, or sunk in what wallowing self-indulgences.

He protested that on the contrary these years had been crowded with hardly supportable acts of God, some of them of an almost medieval savagery.

A space she repeated of seventeen years which he could as guiltily compute as she but which she was not asking him to justify to her, now or ever, neither was she really rebuking him, she said with a gentle glance, since she was *fond* of him, and also she was forgiving and besides it had after all not been really his fault that their affair had ended as it had, she admitted, drooping her pretty eyelids, but she did wish him to know that though in those seventeen years she'd been tempted by other men often, and twice *agonizingly* (she had never told anyone about either of these and never would tell anyone but him, but early in the war this utterly charming Free French attaché had fallen terribly movingly in love with her, the most stormy and haunting siege, and ah such tenderness of desire, he of course desiring but she on her part too, oh she'd *never* been quite so wrung he was so handsome and bereft, and this affair she chronicled for him scene by scene, but he'd been caught on a secret mission to Toulon in 1944 and stood against a wall and shot and she hadn't even the consolation of having made love with him even once and made him happy, she said in grief, taking out a little jewel-studded Louis XVI pillbox, a small capsule from which she washed down with Montrachet, and then later this other, the second husband of one of her three best friends, a *heart*-breakingly attractive Carolinian who'd pursued her with the most intoxicating gaiety for nearly two years, and she described in detail the tender, frustrate, and harrowing course of this adulterous passion too) but in spite of these, in spite of others too at times almost as blissfully devastating as they, as close as they to the ideal exemplar and paradigm of the delicately panting female heart, yet she had nevertheless stayed *faithful* to him, did he realize that? she cried almost angrily, foolishly faithful *thanklessly* faithful, she'd not ever had another affair, so there! or she supposed ever even fallen in love again really, she told him softly, in fact probably he'd spoiled her life for her and he was a pig, she charged, smiling contentedly into his eyes.

During all this he had taken away the trout, which they'd nearly consumed, and carried the plates to the kitchen and brought out dessert plates and the cherry tart with its creamy swags and gadroons, and they had eaten a good part of it and he had additionally eaten a couple of peaches and some green almonds, and then he had brought the coffee out to the table so as not to interrupt her, and they'd drunk that and she had had a Cointreau and he a kirsch, and she had helped him clear the table and rinse-and-stack in the little kitchen as of old; so it turned out that at the moment she called him a pig she happened to be standing so near him as to be as good as in his arms.

Taking the sweet stylish creature into them therefore he begged if he now might know whether all this could by some divine benevolence mean (what he hardly dared hope) that she still did love him (who God knew had never ceased adoring *her*); and when she murmured in happy acquiescence how could he possibly suppose this, so unlikely, so utterly out of the question, resting her forehead on his collarbone where it had rested so many thousands of times, he kissed the elegantly sculptured shaft of her neck where its curve was at its most heavenly and where he remembered it moved her most.

Whereupon clinging to him she whimpered she must go. He said
would she be quiet? when he'd been on the point of reciting for her
(and translating) that couplet of Ovid's that went

ego semper amavi
et si quid faciam nunc quoque quaeris, amo

which he'd render impromptu for her

Always in love till now, till now's been true.
And now? Why, dammy, I'm in love now too.

For like Ovid, he (Nicholas) being a man of sensibility was a damn'
sight more devotedly faithful than the reputation which in mere
feminine manoeuvring she kept gracelessly trying to give him: she'd
plundered his senses twenty years ago once for all and every beat of
her own responding heart must tell her so!—a claim which she
informed him dreamily he must know was false from end to end.

So then they kissed for some time.

Until tenderly taking her mouth away from him she half-said,
" ... mustn't," and opening her eyes to him at last, " ... so untrustworthy," she breathed, her look all soft radiance, lost, lifting her
mouth again for a kiss which this time went on for some while too.

Thus they stood shaken and clinging, in this mild daze; hardly
even practical, vacuous in fact and abandoned; mindlessly sighing
as in time past so many thousands of times; she saying at last
" ... and you've been so long ah Nicholas," in comment on which
he like a fool mumbled the first thing that came into his head, an
amiable "—these damn' people you marry."

At which to his flat astonishment she burst into tears and fled
from him into the basement hall!

"*Now* what in God's name can I have said now!" he groaned
out, chasing after and grabbing her at the foot of the stair, where
while she wept in his arms she absolutely would not look at him or
speak.

"But Victoria!" he implored her, distracted, "Now my *sweetest*
of women!"

Still she wept.

"My darling creature you can't mean to tell me," he havered on
(as she had told him nothing), "that some mere fortuitous
reference like that to your damn' husb— "

"How *could* you!" she raged, stopping her tears instantly.

"But I merely—"

"Just at the most tender—   *Just* when I was so—"

"But in God's thunderstruck name—"

"—heartless taunting rake!" she choked, snatching his handkerchief from his breast-pocket and dabbing in fury.

"But I—"

She shrieked, "Oh when you can't even realize what your selfish grabbing insensitive nature *involves* me in even!" thrusting him off and flying up the stair, and (when he scrambled after her) flinging his handkerchief back down at his disconcerted face. "Have I no life of my own then?" she raved from the top step, whirling upon him panting.

"Now my utterly blessed woman what earthly elaborate disorder *is* this?" he begged, jarring to a halt a step below her, quailing.

"And when you don't even know what you ask!"

" 'Not know'!"

"Oh you put me off so!"

"But I *love* you goddammit!" he shouted.

" 'Love me,' when you've not even the most doltish retarded notion—   How *could* you misunderstand me for seventeen whole years!"

He moaned, "My darling will you merely once listen to me at all?" stretching out his hands in what seemed entreaty, though where they came to rest was her sleek waist.

"When everything I ever felt about you—"

"But that's exactly the point I've—"

"Why, you can't even see what thinking you love me as you used to will merely do to me!" she upbraided him, great blue eyes filling with tears of sheer reproof.

"Are you in some mad contriving feminine imposture going to pretend that from the moment I first laid eyes on you, there at your baby sister's wedding," he cried in the most moving unhappiness, "without the intervention of a single day—Victoria my one darling among women I don't need to swear it, you *know* it, every lovely inch of you knows it!" he declaimed.

So she gazed at him more reasonably.

And in fact next said, "But my darling it isn't that I doubt you, or anyhow not really, though of course you heartlessly lie to me constantly," she gently regretted, taking one of his hands from her waist to hold it against her cheek, "but when I had to organize some sort of life for myself when you left me, you must *see*!"

"But my love I 'left' you only because you—"

This tactless topic she condoningly hushed by instantly putting her fingers over his lips, while conceding, "Yes, and this autumn who'd merely *believe* now he'll be a huge sixth-former," before continuing, "But Nicholas you do have to see what loving you all over again will do to my responsibilities if I were for one minute to let you have your selfish way."

"My angel—"

"And simply upset everything I've lived with, oh Nicholas my whole ordered life all these years and my delightful son and my husb— my house," she ran sadly on, stroking his temple apologetically with a fingertip, "why, simply all these peaceful family emotions I'm used to, my poor old darling. Only now you want to bully me into letting you sweep everything away and how *can* I, how could I stand it if I let everything I felt for you— And I *never* felt about anyone what I did for you, oh caro look your hair's getting gray," she sniffed in misery.

"But just by god had it cut again too!" he snickered, remembering; and with a snort of laughter took her back in his arms—where after a moment she had the complaisance to giggle.

"Ahhhh think of it all though!" he exulted tenderly. "There you were at your sister's wedding in that damn' receiving line, I couldn't even touch your hand!"

"Well, you did, you brought me that first glass of champagne; *so* noticing, Nicholas."

"Looked thirsty," he smirked, reasonably.

"So sweet."

"More than your damn' husband did for you!"

"Oh the way you *looked* at me when you came up with my champagne, oh darling I never felt so undefendable and I didn't even know who you were."

"My god Victoria how d'you think *I* felt!"

"We fell in love with each other right there, in front of everybody on earth, you never realized that?" she told him soberly.

"Your face gave everything away."

".....I know."

"You knew *then*!"

"Well you were *lovely*-looking!" she cried in happy extenuation; and suddenly in immemorial flight slipping from his hands and (when neighing her name he lunged after her) seized his hands and kissed the heel of the thumb of one of them with little silly kisses, while he declaimed (rather more in the manner of, say, the Earl of Rochester than in his own) that he wished the whole round world were as entirely hers as he was, now or ever, for then she would have no reason to complain of anything!

But "oh Nicholas, oh we mustn't, I can't," she mumbled amorously, giving him a great kiss; and then pulling herself away fluttered along the hall and into the front drawing-room.

Here however when he caught her she utterly handed herself over, every charming inch, for the whole heaven-sent eternity of a dozen heart-beats.

So when she then again began to struggle, how could he help ranting (in words as straight from the heart as under Charles II or any other king by god) that she was the most afflicting fair creature in the world! for whence came this peevish prudence that hourly advised her concerning him how 'dangerous' it was to be kind to the one man on earth who loved her best?

"Ah never!" she cried in sheer laughing happiness, and fled him.

What, was he to be permitted to gaze upon the miracle she was, yet forever have the miracle she might do him forbidden him? he chased her proclaiming, with a shout of laughter; for could she not pick her deserving serv^t, himself, and place her kindness *there*?—an act so lofty as would show the greatness of her spirit, and distinguish her in love, as she was in all things else, from womankind. And still laughing caught her and kissed her, a long long kiss.

Until she again took that heavenly mouth away from him sighing and quivering, mournfully whispering, " ... is awful," eyes one unending confiding smile; and then with one more flurry of quick pouted kisses (nyim-nyim-nyim-nyim) escaped him again, in little laughing sighing rushes from room to room, he now delightedly crying could she reproach to him that he had no ways, save words, to express that love to her, yet uncivilly still refuse him all means, save words, to acquaint her with it? for was he to have thought her more of an angel than he now found her a woman? and ran her down in the back drawing-room against the curve of the piano at last, whereupon she nuzzled and cooed and femalized at him in general.

And let him lead her to the foot of the stairs, where she gave him a long kiss. "Oh how I want you when I mustn't even *consider* you!" she lamented, kissing him again, blue eyes melted. "And when it is so impossible oh darling," kissing him once more, in a gale of sighs.

And in a perfect haze of love let him take her up his stairs.

So, then, in a kind of wild calm at last, breathless with rushing and with laughter, both of them, on in, to his elegant rosewood bed—both of them having after all, for hours, known exactly what they were doing.

He was working his contented way through his mail next day between tender attempts to phone his Victoria (who kept being out: "Corinna's gone with all her brokers maying," he muttered, a line he'd after all written to her and no other, however many years ago it now was), working his way through a grotesque mail in fact, a snapshot of loquat trees and a dirty impluvium, endorsed "Here is nothing of great interest old boy but at least everyone keeps his meals down, how good God is," and a Class of 1931 Reunion announcement captioned in blackletter A Clean Old Man Never Decays, not to mention other letters equally disfigured by signs of wide-spread and various world disorder, including a manuscript-size communication from his wife's lawyers which he merely bundled off to his own (who were the same men anyhow), when Melissa rang up.

"Now daddy what *is* this, what unpredictable thing have you done to Morgan!"

Taken flat aback, he uttered a resounding cry.

"Well daddy it's *Melissa*: I said 'to Morgan'; I mean darling is the connection bad or something? because what have you been doing to her?"

"*I* done!"

"So you did perfectly well understand all the time!"

"How's that?" he bayed.

"Well daddy I do think it's not only irresponsible but just *provoking* of you, I mean forgive me and all, sweetie, but after all here she just *is*!"

"But dammit what if she is!"

"But she's *hysterical* from you!"

"She's *what*?"

"Oh dearest don't yell; hysterical."

"Who says this?"

"I'm just *telling* you, goodness! she's been here in my hands this whole half-morning crying her heart out over your treatment of her and I do think it's utterly pathetic!"

He roared, "May I interrupt this flood of womanly pity long enough to make out—"

"Daddy *please*!"

"Yes but what am I accused of dammit!"

"Dearest I *wasn't* accusing you; why, what a thing to say; it was Morgan."

"Then what's Morgan accus— "

"Well goodness how do *I* know, I called you to *ask*! Daddy she's just too upset to say, except you were terribly unfeeling and unkind and as good as—"

" 'Unfeeling'!"

"Well she's so incoherent and sobbing, what *did* you do to her?"

" 'Do,' by god Melissa on your own insistence I took her to the Iridium Room and what's more I additionally gave a damn' good lunch if you want to know to the squalling little she-brat!"

This produced a shocked silence. Finally she said, "Well but *daddy*." And then, "Well sweetie all I can say is, that isn't exactly *her* story!"

"I don't by god doubt *that* in the least!"

"But *something* upset her, you will admit?"

On this, he choked.

"What, dearest? because if I am trying to merely make some sense of all this it's on *your* account daddy after all!"

He said in an attempt at a lighter tone, "Now Melissa the plain apodeictic fact is nobody is very sensible," but she paid no attention to this truth, on the contrary went on:

"When I suppose with Toby off at sea again and *no* letters, I know you're just a man and don't know about things daddy but girls get perfectly *panicky*, anyhow if in frantic loneliness or whatever she went around to see you *of course* it's your fault! why, you took her dancing and then you fed her this very good lunch as you just admitted yourself!"

"My dear Melissa the child hardly—"

"Because at any rate she admittedly did go round to see you for whatever reason, you won't deny!"

"By god didn't she!"

"So sweetie I do think you might see your responsibilities a little more promptly don't you? And go soothingly around to see her and apologize! Because I'm taking her back to her apartment, I can't just go *on* having her weeping here, goodness! Because is it really too outlandishly difficult for you just to step into a taxi when you haven't anything actually to do anyhow? and go make it up with the poor bruised bereft thing! And like a sweet *not* yell? but just go appease her. Instead of brutalize and terrify, daddy!"

So if the man was not to yell at his precious daughter, what could he do.

—Even though goddammit how was *his* conduct toward that unhelpless little seductress of his "irresponsible" but not hers toward him! a question he'd by heaven like to propound to people who think answers answer! Such for example as that Edwardian lawyer of his with his comfortable fifteen-stone felicitousnesses ("After all, no one, surely now, Nick old man, more aware than yourself? Of the pitfalls? Furor ille revisit and so forth, how's it go. Girls being, after all, flighty veering little things at best! And these first virginal fancies, Nick, after all!") and Time the Healer and so forth till doomsday—when the plain fact was that the only course for a decent man was both to take her and not to take her!

Whom in a word loved or unloved he must equally destroy, if one cared to use these stately terms!

"—and let him who is without luck among ye cast the first die!" he snarled; and sent the man for a taxi.

—On the whole better not take her flowers: might well just become dried keepsakes; keep memories needlessly alive.

But then, *no* by heaven, for had le bon Dieu created the touching, the charming memory of woman only for psychiatry to prevent its filling itself with the sweet woe it cherished most? so first thing he did was lay his flowers on his young love's bed, though her room was in such sad darkness he barely made out where she lay.

And sending her dithering maid away and pulling up a chair to her bedside he said now poor little sweet what *was* this.

From a shadowy tent of silence her hand slid out and sought his, which it weakly clung to; but she said nothing.

So he solicitously prodded but *what* then, for wouldn't she say? Because he went on to assure her here he was, d'she see? as she'd asked that he be; if she'd take her pretty nose out of those suffocating pillows and look at him she'd see for herself he was not only here but here from the tenderest *concern* for her.

But what at last from the muffling depths of her bed she miserably whispered was that she loved him.

He said but—

Loved him, and a woman's only life was love; and then her voice died piteously away.

He said he knew. He *knew*. Nevertheless—

Concern was the word he'd used but what he'd meant was pity. So she was going away, to spare him. Even possibly to a sanitarium. But not burden him again. She was going to be what he wanted her to, responsible. All she could do was say adieu. With her lips; for with her heart, never.

Why, he said, she had her whole young life before her, what kind of talk was this! with in fact only one thing not in her power, viz., to reward any man in the world with half so much sweetness as she had thrown away on his worthless and irrelevant self.

She wanted to die. She was so worn. But she would not. Truly not. If only because then he might blame himself. When it was not his fault that she loved him so. She could never blame him. She could only love him.

He tried saying now what was so damn' charming about *him*? even if some sweet creature had the indulgence to let a man see she thought so, still the plain truth was— Would she bear for a moment with a Classical analogy? for take the Iliad: the Iliad it often appeared was like a ballet, matched heroes dancing forward at each other in opposing pairs to fling their antiphonal taunts and spears, then dancing back, and then after a choral movement of the ordinary infantry another pair coming on, another pas de deux; and this he said was how it often seemed to be with love, the shafts of woman's transfixing beauty ran him through, their sighs answering his antiphonally in turn, and if it was ever-changing and new still was it each time any the less utterly a death? and so there it was.

She replied, but now so low he could barely hear her, that a woman never forgot the man who first made her feel she was a woman, there was nobody like him for her ever, but her love for him was more than merely this, he *was* the love of her life, that was all, even now she had renounced him; and if he was shallow and she loved him more deeply than he had ever loved her, or loved any woman, or could love, that was her fate; her doom; he could love one woman, as he said, and then in time another, and love the second as much as he had the first, but *her* heart she had given him for life, and she had only one to give. And how was she merely to get through the fifty years more, the half-century, that he kept telling her she had every reason to look forward to, with no more of him than this? she ended brokenly, beginning as in sheer weakness to cry.

Well poor devil what could he or any man say.

But presently she stopped; and then she said, sniffling, here was her diary, and from somewhere under her in the tumbled linen she pushed a warm grubby little volume toward him. Because he was to take it. It was the chronicle of her love. He was to take it as a last act of ritual kindness since he would not take her. For it broke off on the day—   Well, he would see, because the last entry she had made would tell him *how* she loved him, no longer the girl she had been that now lost November afternoon when she'd come into his library from the stables to tea and seen him and known her destiny but like the *woman* her loving him had made her. For this much honor at least he could do her, to read what she had set down. He must promise to. This was all she any longer sought.

He stammered out that the warmth, the sweetness, of her imagination—why, what could be more understandable? and this honest attachment—   And yet no woman could be more aware of the pitfalls, surely, than herself? Ah but dammit he'd not have the insensibility to moralize at her when certainly none of this could be forgotten by *him* by heaven, not ever, her beauty, her lovely impulsive—

But she gasped, now crying bitterly, oh kiss her and go.

So he went, gulping; her diary clenched still warm from her in his hand. And walked heavily to Park Avenue and then downtown, on and on through the early-summer brilliance of afternoon, sighing and cast down, the whole sad dilemma an insoluble damn' shame. And all because of *his* decision, that poor little sweet a mere turning point! and so, helplessly, at last (muttering he by god *must* be suffering an elemental change if he walked out of a pretty girl's bedroom for her own good!) hailed a cab to take him home. Where he finally read her diary's last entry:

> Charme de l'amour, oh this enchanted certainty that I have found the one being I was created for; this sudden light of day over everything—and what was mystery, so clear! this unsuspected worth in the merest nothings; these swift hours whose details by their very sweetness elude my memory yet leave this long furrow of happiness through my heart; such bliss in your presence, and even when you are away, such hope—

But hadn't he read something like this somewhere or other before?

Soon he would sail.

But meanwhile his Victoria now had the complaisance to find time for him often in her book, he having as she said to be looked after, *seen* to.

Thus for example "...........," this angel wordlessly murmured one happy dusk; drowsy, entangled; in a word all his again, they being in the great dim rosewood bed at the time. And he, in agreeable stupor, sprawled all anyhow, in time groaned out amiably into her shoulder what might have been an answering "........mm."

This conversation then died in contentment away.

Until at length in a torpid voice he got out, " ... at *this* age, ah Victoria, to say 'I love you.' "

She made some fond and languid sound.

"Knowing now what it means," he yawned.

Her knees slid, slackly hugging him. These lovers then shifted position a bit, deprecatingly; then once again lay there, now comfortable, this dialogue too stalled. Or as if there were no language in the world.

But at long last he sighed, and, eyes now open, appeared even to think. In due course rolled up onto his big elbow, to where she no longer blurred on him, and delivered himself of droning reminiscence: by what towers, what ancient streets, down what narrowing marble geometries, ah by what fountains, had not her image turned to him, smiling and silent; then he lounged down to where, for this, she let him have her sleepy mouth as he pleased again.

He mumbled, "Of all our memories, which."

In their private twilight she opened her eyes to him, gazing, wordless and grave.

"Then which, Victoria."

But as at some softer question, in pause, she mused, bending this long sweet fathomless look on him still.

"All these years, snared like this in the tender net of you."

Her eyes closed.

"Until now we're here by god," he concluded vaguely, and patting his angel he yawned.

"Here, and after all that," he drowsily expanded. "After all that shared and inextricable history. Yet now it still goes on!" So she drifted closer against him, settling.

"Which I suppose by god then," he went on in a different tone, "is why your sweet fussing sex is everlastingly engaged in making us feel 'responsible' for you, isn't it! Hand yourselves over batting those great reproachful eyes, and if this all-of-you isn't important enough for a— Now will you not flounce away pouting dammit?" he commanded, rolling after her. "I said, if the insensate hog does nothing but add you to his inventory— Turn *over* here!" he cried, grabbing and uncoiling her.

So she let herself be re-arranged to suit him.

"Ahhh what's all your mad flittery manoeuvring for anyway," he laughed in pure affection, "if not that you want us to *accept* the fact of what you are, is that it? the whole wild vertigo of you, why dammy for all I know you'll decide your feelings are hurt if I haven't demanded *you* get a divorce from your damn'— Thought of *that* before you thought I had by heaven didn't I?" he snorted, for in the gloom she had opened her eyes to him again, and she was faintly smiling.

"So I put *up* with your moods, d'you see? if only so you'll feel spoiled to your heart's content," he explained. "And if I didn't occasionally yell at you how'd you be sure I took you seriously, isn't that how you want it, my slumbering Macchiavellian angel? Are you listening to me at all?"

For her eyes had closed once more, and in the dusky air, as from down some footfall passageway, came no more than the breathed echo of a reply.

He stroked her, grumbling tenderly, "If we're not willing to be that much accountable, I suppose you don't feel like a woman do you. Lacking the final proof. That one unstatable attestation to what you were born to be. Is that why you love me then?" he demanded of her shadowy face. "Because I do by god accept putting up with you, you delectable thing?" and hauled her into his arms.

Where, though for all anybody could tell she was already a good two-thirds asleep, she lovingly let him do with her as he pleased.

In a country-summer sunset now a mere nightfall dim gold, all gilding gone, Melissa and once more Melissa's hostess sat murmuring, wayworn, on the plinth of the sundial in its darkening lawn, ivory in their evening silks; as if spent, night upon them; the sweet friend fretting "—so love I am driven *mad*, then," quivering.

"Mm."

"Ah who wouldn't be left maddened? when how can I even wait till I meet him in Italy yet here is this utter quandary *where*!"

"Poor love."

"Because if I go with him to this lovely stealthy out-of-the-way little place he wants it won't sound like turismo even to Sam! Who I'll have to phone every night to make sure merely! Yet we *have* to keep away from places we'd run into people we know in and then anyway who wants to see tiresome Sights? when what will I even be able to think of but him, I mean Liss where *are* we to go!" she lamented, drooping.

"Dear I do see!"

"Mi fa impazzire!"

"Ma dove che sia—"

"No but I'm just *impaired* by it all! and all Patrick does is laugh, he says why not simply some huge cool dim cinquecento bedroom then in for example Siena and *stay* in bed! when he ought to know he'd very soon just start thinking about food!"

Melissa cried lightly, "Well pity on *him*!" in what may have been their college-era dialect.

"No but when all I want to know is what he'd *truly* like, why can't he see?"

"Sweetie I thought your great angel of a husband—"

"Ptah he'll say he's tied up in Geneva all August. Or half. Oh Lissa how can I even begin to wait!"

Melissa yawned "Thee must just possess thy soul in patience," quoting her great-grandmother at her.

"But how can I, oh how dismal you are, when for this whole month or almost I can authentically live with Patrick and look *after* him and not just play house in these sheer agonies of having to part in a few sad vanishing hours, so rushing and gone."

"Yes you said."

"And I *never* felt responsible for anybody like this before," she wailed to the gathering night. "Oh one's parents were so lucky, just affairs affairs and never bother their heads, when Lissa what is there merely to think about seriously but this!"

"Mm."

"And Patrick *admits*! Or anyhow as applying to women he says he admits. That what else is there to think of ever but love, I mean. Except I think he feels every agonizing bit the way I do, dearest he *must*, or d'you think? for example only two times ago he said had I any notion how hellish it was? because he said how could I!"

"So bliss then."

"So *bliss* then, well exactly! If he does mean it, that is. But he *does* Lissa! Or don't you think," she whimpered.

"Dear love *mmm*."

But the friend cried in hopelessness, "Oh though how can I look after him Liss when it isn't even as if I could look *after* him, when what else were we made to do but be with them, oh I endlessly despair!"

"Love, how sad."

"Ah and he's so darling, so amusing," that one mourned, bereft. "Simply the things he'll say, I mean he's just constantly tossing these wildly unexpected sardonic epigrams *off* Lissa, he just impromptu made up that phrase 'as un-American as *good* apple pie.' "

"*Mm.*"

"And the last time we were at the St. Regis they served him what he said was this *perfectly* cynical incompetent duck-and-olives, he says if they don't give up catering to Texans *he*'s going to stop going there, and he called the maître d'hôtel over and said to him, 'Your chef missed his calling, whatever it was,' well just *demolishing*! Oh I love him I *love* him he's teaching me to drink those horrible Italian aperitifs or did I tell you," she ended, gazing into the night, in happy dream.

But Melissa airily stretched her young arms high, saying yawning, absently, after all what could one expect? when how could anyone after all know!

Then the floodlights came abruptly on over the rich terrace and it was what her father would have called their damn' husbands. Who yelled out across were they coming to get a drink for God's sake or weren't they.

ﻌﺪﺉﺒﻌ

One hot mid-afternoon at last anybody who was still in town came down to Nicholas's ship to say bon voyage.

And it might have been the Thirties all over again, his cabin jammed, flowers everywhere and the most agreeable urban din, Victoria's man eeling his way through the hubbub with the champagne and the usual horde of well-wishing contemporaries in full cry, classmates admen whatnot, even his lawyer from Philadelphia again with dockets of last-minute-be-on-the-safe-side stifling stuff to be signed; and then too (and pleased and touched him) a random three or four of his New York nieces and nephews and whoever they'd severally had lunch with that day, the girls sleek as colts in their summery dresses and a couple of them calling him *sir* southern-style while drooping their unmaidenly eyelids at him; and presently Melissa too, racing in out of breath, with some smooth well-mannered young giant he'd never set eyes on in his life who *sir*'d him with that tiresome Yale deference while Melissa conveyed the most dutiful best wishes of her husband, who hadn't been able to get away from his bank, absolutely greatest regret of his life; and finally Victoria, looking not in the least as if she were due in Paris herself in a fortnight and would ring him the moment she got in. So he grumbled in affection now he *wished* she'd have the sensibility to reconsider and let him motor down and meet her properly and comfortably at Cherbourg, they'd drive for lunch for instance to Caen, where he'd once had the best coq au vin of his life, then up to Paris in easy stages, spending the night in that beech forest around Lyons why not? for what if it wasn't the direct route, was she going to deny him the pleasure of the first night he'd ever spent in the Forêt de Lyons with the woman he loved?

But she said ssshhh, now who was that with Melissa.

"How would I know a thing like that, missed his name, generation of mumblers in *my* view," he complained.

"Then he came with her? so good-looking, Nicholas!"

"Of course I'm persuaded she must be out of her silly mind!" he burst out in great unhappiness.

And when Mrs. Barclay opened her eyes wide at this, muttered in raging explanation, "Abruptly been stricken, if you must know, with this infuriating conviction I'm being presented with a new damn' son-in-law!"

"Oh Nicholas no!"

"An *outrage!*" he fumed, as she turned to see for herself and murmuring " ... not Melissa surely" took in Melissa and her young man in one instantaneous assize.

"Even wrong side of the blanket, how do *I* know," Nicholas told her in dejection.

"Now my old darling he obviously does adore her!"

"By god he'd better!"

"*She* I must say looks entirely self possessed."

He made some hollow maundering sound.

"She is a sweet, Nicholas."

"Well, evidently, yes, what man could help himself I suppose," he conceded, sunk.

"Why a perfect darling!" she sang in encouragement. "And in point of fact of course he's terribly attractive-looking."

"Whatever that's got to do with it!"

"Oh Nicholas what utter—"

He snarled, "Ah well, young and healthy enough I suppose, yes!"

"Though hardly more than a child actually is she," Mrs. Barclay at once acknowledged.

"Well exactly by god!"

"Your oldest or is she Nicholas too."

"My own daughter!" he cried morosely, staring.

"Your first actually?"

He grunted in gloom, draining his glass. "Though what difference?" he declaimed in valediction. "Walk out on you don't they? Of age or not? One after another! Leaving me knee-deep among these unpredicted ruins!"

But smiling into his eyes she gently teased, "Now old darling don't be an old stupid."

"See how it is?" he snorted, making some sort of bogus face, "show a natural affection for a pretty daughter and every woman in ear-shot begins denigrating my intelligence."

"Nicholas haven't you ever thought what my own sweet apoplectic father would have said, and *done* to you darling! if he'd once had the faintest notion—"

"Well, then, why, you're a terrible damn' sex, aren't you?" he decided to agree, beginning to smile back. "Ah well," he went on, more cheerfully, "it's what comes of letting one's daughters marry any young man that happens to take their silly fancy," he ended, even beginning to laugh.

Here however his lawyer worked his weighty way through the uproar and started holding these dockets up against the cabin wall for him to sign one after another, affably bawling his full-phrased enucleation of each in turn into his ear, for example the sheer *extra* papers because what had his Bank's treasurer done but slump to the pavement in Chestnut Street not forty-eight hours before and die before they'd even got a doctor to him, *shockingly* sudden thing, poor stuffy devil, member of all his own clubs, man he'd yelled at five days a week for twenty-odd years, man in a word from his own well-fed well-brought-up decent dying generation, to whom by god there was still a residual meaning in Domesday Book's ancient cadastral *quantum silvae quantum prati* (but now co-parceners of what moss-hung and abandoned avenues, what crumbling porticoes) and it made his heart heavy to think he'd had to yell at him as he had; so they discussed a proper successor. Then they began working their way through the second brief-case and he signed and signed.

Except that, through the river of well-read legal prose, he kept hearing some discountenancing young whelp or other just within earshot in the gay pandemonium behind him muttering (to some girl, he presumed) first something about "the little cloud of angels surrounding you," a nice enough phrase, but next thing he knew followed in a guarded carnal undertone by "even these damned eight inches away from your arms!" to which (and at his very shoulder if you please!) came her teasing little music-box laugh of delighted reply.

The unseen damn' boy panted, "Oh my *loveliest* angel!"

"Oh sweetie be careful!"

"Tomorrow afternoon too? Please *please*?"

"So hongish, ssshh," she tantalized him, in adenoidal, sounding amorous.

The wretched children then began mumbling unintelligibly. Until the boy's voice rose in outrage to the hoarse whisper "—your husband, when I want you!"

"Sweet."

"All of you! All the time!"

"Or do you sweetie, because I can't always think you do."

"*What*, when hardly an hour ago we were—"

"So anulnerous," she cooed, "so wingèd!"

At this they both snickered extravagantly. "So termly san," she giggled; and they were off again. Until from deep in some private joke he said, "Who wants to get on first base anyhow?"

"So *lonely*!" —and they snickered wildly this time for a good half-minute.

While all about them the unheeding company bayed in its brightest party tone.

But when Nicholas turned round at last from signing, the couple, whoever, were already lost among those salvoes of oblivious sound.

Anyway half the company was rustily talking French by this time, it having been found that the girl of one of his nephews was not southern at all but from Paris. Also, by this time nobody was any longer tasting his drink, just drinking it. Melissa moreover buttonholed him and conveyed the most dutiful wishes, the very sincerest best regards possible, if only he could know, of her husband, did he know he hadn't been able even to get *away*! Then the all-ashore gong began sounding and all the girls except the girl from Paris (who however had turned out to be Swiss) kissed him languishing good-byes and off everybody went, chattering in English again.

And last, at the very gangway, his sweet Victoria kissed him, mistily; and for just that instant clung to him, wordless; and was gone.

Presently everybody else had gone too, for long before dusk they had to be at sea.

And when at dinner he stared agreeably about for some engaging creature to pick up next day (*eat* with her anyhow), there seemed to be no one. Though in any case, he at once virtuously remembered, he had now changed his spots, hadn't he! Worn down as he was after everything to the man he was here and now.

Why, even the thought of Arabella Hobbes hardly crossed his mind!

And so eventually out then under the ocean night with its soft wind from home, to lean in dim starlight on the sports-deck rail, his full-fed gaze toward France; away; alone. "Or alone for this hour anyhow," he said aloud to those dark leagues of sea ahead, to Europe in fact, in declamatory apostrophe.

So not even Arabella; no. If only because Neuilly and the Place Vendôme weren't far enough apart geographically to keep separate two pretty women who'd run into each other in the rue du Faubourg St. Honoré in any case. And fancy at his age organizing a shuttle anyhow! Even apart from such sighing tangential questions as whether memories were ever what one is after.

And besides, as said, hadn't he changed?

For if there are no answers (if virtue is for example not an acquired characteristic; or conversely if when leopards change their spots it is not their spots they change), if there are no answers there are still perorations, and "Have I then mended my ways for *you* Victoria goddammit?" he cried aloud, and began to laugh; and waving a tamed hand westward to her through the dark seaward rush of the ocean night, proclaimed in final self-approbation, "So then onward and upward by god!"

And turning aft went below.

To where, in the companionway to which he was affably descending, life comfortably settled, all virtue scheduled at last, there stood waiting (here and now), her little scarlet lip quivering, her eyes enormous with terror and determination, his sweet besieger, his suppliant, his captive, his very loving stowaway, his Morgan.

A NOTE ON THE TYPE

THE TEXT OF THIS BOOK was set in a face called Times Roman, designed by STANLEY MORISON for *The Times* (London), and first introduced by that newspaper in 1932. Among typographers and designers of the twentieth century, Stanley Morison has been a strong forming influence, as typographical adviser to the English Monotype Corporation, as a director of two distinguished English publishing houses, and as a writer of sensibility, erudition, and keen practical sense.

Printed on Caresse Laid
paper made by
Monadnock Paper Company

Printed and bound by
The Haddon Craftsmen, Inc.,
Scranton, Pa.

Display type and binding design
by Holly McNeely.